'Stay off the mountain, or I'll report you to the sheriff,' he warned in a harsher tone than any he'd used previously with her.

'I don't respond to threats,' she felt compelled to inform him, hearing the haughtiness in her tone.

'You're on my turf here. You'll do well to remember that.'

Memories of last night's kisses flooded Alison without notice. Her eyes were irresistibly drawn to his lips, now compressed into a thin line of disapproval. Last night they had been mobile and sensuous, enticing her to follow his lead into passionate play.

Hunger swept through her, flooding her with needs stronger than she'd ever known. This fierce mountain man had opened a void inside her, one she hadn't been fully aware of until two days ago. It was very disturbing.

'Well?' he demanded.

'I'm sorry. What did you say?'

He looked as if he could grind glass with his teeth. 'I want your word that you'll do as I request.'

For once.

His eyes, locked on hers, admitted there was something different between them, something neither had encountered before. They blazed with blue fire, igniting the ready embers in her.

Her breath fluttered to her throat and seemed to die. She couldn't breathe, couldn't look away…

Available in April 2004 from Silhouette Special Edition

Something to Hide
LAURIE PAIGE

SILHOUETTE®
SPECIAL EDITION™

*First published in Great Britain 2004
Silhouette Books, Eton House, 18-24 Paradise Road,
Richmond, Surrey TW9 1SR*

© Olivia M. Hall 2003

ISBN 0 373 60155 7

23-0404

*Printed and bound in Spain
by Litografia Rosés S.A., Barcelona*

For Wendy and Sayde and Stacey and Josie…
with apologies for the name switch!
Love, Aunt L.

LAURIE PAIGE

has won many awards for her romances, but one of the
best rewards for writing, she says, comes from her
readers. Some write to share their experiences, some
to share recipes, some to report they grew up in the
story location. Legends and folklore, as well as off-
the-beaten-path places, are also part of the fun…and
can liven things up for intrepid heroines and exasperated heroes!

Dear Reader,

Living less than a hundred miles from the Pacific Ocean, I have to head east to get to most places, such as Kentucky for a family reunion, or Colorado for the Romance Writers of America conference. I view all trips as wonderful opportunities to explore places for romantic stories. My husband is used to my adding hundreds of miles to a journey because a name on a map caught my eye. While he fishes for trout, I look for angles and hooks to catch a love story.

I discovered the Seven Devils Mountains on such an excursion. Who could resist He Devil and She Devil mountains? As we travelled through the region, and both sides of Hells Canyon—it was a lo-o-ng way down!—stories began to buzz through my head. When visiting old churches and graveyards, or stopping by the local Forestry Service offices, I always find a gold-mine of information on families, legends, plants and geology.

Uncle Nick is my idea of everyone's favourite uncle and a loose composite of three longtime residents of one of the many towns tucked away into those devilish hills. They were having morning coffee in a tiny diner where we stopped for breakfast. After listening to their conversation (okay, I admit it; I'm an inveterate eavesdropper), I soon joined in and asked about a million questions. That people answer them always amazes my hubby. But not me. I find wonderful people wherever we go.

Well, I have to pack. It's off to Kentucky, but first there's this place in Montana, near the Canadian border, that I'd like to explore…

Laurie Paige

Chapter 1

A stranger in a small town was always cause for curiosity and speculation among the local population. A lone female hiking in the Seven Devils Mountains of Idaho, some of the roughest backcountry in the U.S., was an anomaly not to be ignored.

From his mining site, Travis Dalton observed the woman through the powerful lens of his binoculars as she stopped, consulted a map, gazed in the direction of He-Devil Mountain, then set out along the trail she was following, which was hardly more than a rabbit track.

She was either lost or stupid to be wandering alone through the mountains with nothing but the map, a light jacket tied around her waist and a bottle of water hooked to the waistband of her jeans. He opted for lost *and* stupid.

After a couple of minutes, he decided her goal was to get to the top of the limestone ridge. If she crossed it, she would be in the watershed of Hells Canyon, the deepest gorge in the continental U.S., cut by the Snake River as it plunged along the border separating Oregon and Idaho.

Why the devil would she be heading into the hills?

It was none of his business, and frankly, he didn't give a damn, as someone had once said. He wasn't Sir Galahad, out to rescue some female from her own folly.

But she was encroaching on his territory and he resented the hell out of that.

Okay, so she was on national forestland, not the ranch, but nobody in her right mind wandered through the region as if on a field trip. This was wilderness. Deep wilderness. Puma country. Bears, too.

In fact, he'd thought it might be the big mama cat on the prowl when he'd spotted movement a couple of times on the upland trail. That's when he'd gotten out the binoculars. It didn't pay to let down your guard, not if a person wanted to survive out here.

The woman stopped again and rubbed a hand across her forehead, a gesture conveying fatigue and worry.

Uneasiness ruffled the abyss of calm inside him. With a muttered curse, he reminded himself he came to the mountains to get away from people. This was his time to be alone, to escape his family's concern and their everlasting prying into his emotions.

The chasm stilled, becoming one with the endless darkness that was his soul. He preferred it that way. Two years had passed since he'd had any feelings. He'd buried those along with his wife and unborn child.

Grimly he watched the woman as she checked the map once more, his mind automatically recording a description as if he might have to write up a police report later or describe her to his brother, who was with the sheriff's department.

Mid to late twenties. Five feet six inches. Hundred and twenty pounds. Light-brown to dark-blond hair. Gray or green eyes?

She glanced behind her, then all around. She looked directly his way, startling him as her eyes seemed to meet his through the spy-glass lens, an expression of despair in the smoky-green depths.

As if in sympathy with the woman's troubles, the darkness stirred again, burning him in its fiery void, the *nothingness* that could only be kept at bay through hard work or a resolute anger.

He focused on the intruder once more. In addition to the despair, he picked up more than a hint of determination in her manner. The question was: what the heck was she determined to do? It was suicide to be up here with no supplies.

A harsh ripple of anguish tore through him at the thought, reminding him of a time when he'd thought life wasn't worth the effort of living. Sometimes he still felt that way; however, the woman didn't seem bent on self-destruction.

She folded the map and stuffed it into her pocket. He noted she didn't have a compass or one of the global positioning system devices all the yuppies carried these days. At least with a GPS, she could have punched in location coordinates so she could find her way back to wherever she came from.

His mood went from black to blacker, and he considered getting back to work. She seemed to know what she was doing.

At that moment, a breeze stirred the new spring growth on the trees above her and a ray of sunlight flooded her in an aura of brightness, freezing him in place.

It was as if she'd been gilded. Her hair shimmered with golden highlights, a secret treasure hidden among the shining waves. Her skin became alabaster, so translucent it seemed as if the light came from within, as if she were made of some magical substance containing only sunshine and fairy dust in equal portions.

He reached out instinctively to touch her, to gather a handful of the magic for himself. She heaved a visible sigh, then moved on. He lowered the binoculars and realized his hands were trembling.

Turning abruptly, he stored the mattock and spade in the shallow cave where he was working a thin vein of gold and replaced the binoculars in the case. He'd known from the moment he'd spotted her that he would have to check out the situation. Even he couldn't leave a woman to become crow bait in the wilderness.

So he'd have to see if he could help her out, but he didn't have to like it.

After a quick glance at the slant of the late-afternoon sun, he figured he wouldn't get back to the mine that day. He hoisted the day pack. It was better to have emergency equipment on hand than to wish for it a mile up the trail.

Settling the pack and the rifle over his shoulders, he started out, aware of the fading light and knowing there was no way to rescue the woman before dark. He would have to take her to his base camp for the night. Beyond that, he didn't want to think.

Muttering a curse, he quickened his pace. Where the devil did the woman think she was going, heading up an old game trail that eventually petered out deep in the Payette National Forest?

She was almost five miles from the logging road, at least forty miles from town. Since she was above him on the trail with a good quarter-mile lead, he'd be lucky if they made it back to camp and didn't have to sleep in the shelter of a tree. He preferred the relative comfort of his tent.

While the days had been warm and sunny for a week, the night temperature could drop into the freezing range. May was as unpredictable as any month during the spring or fall when the weather patterns were changing.

The anger flared. He needed this time alone, pitting his strength against the mountain until he was too tired to lift the pick. The fatigue erased the memories.

Forcing himself to the present, shaking his head at the human capacity for stupidity, he followed the woman. He was more and more puzzled by her actions as she picked her way farther into the mountains. She didn't act lost. She acted like a person with a mission.

Several possibilities came to mind. As a volunteer deputy, he'd agreed to keep an eye out for some squatters. The local ranchers were complaining about cattle being slaughtered in the field, most of the meat left to rot while steaks and roasts were removed from the carcass. His task was to gather information and/or evidence of such a group actually being in the area.

There were also paramilitarists who occasionally invaded the hills. They played war games with paint balls, but they might use bullets if they wanted a fresh beefsteak for dinner one night.

Keeping tabs on the wilderness wasn't as difficult as most people thought. There was only one main road into the mountains, plus a few nearly impassable logging cuts. Hiking trails followed the winding paths of the local wildlife along creeks. There weren't many of those, either.

Was this woman one of the squatters or with a gang? If so, it was the first time he'd seen her.

Instead of a rescue, maybe he'd better see where she was going and if anyone was meeting her. He slowed his pace a bit. Wearing an old camouflage shirt, he had only to stand still and most people wouldn't notice him if they gave a quick glance over their shoulder. She'd done that a couple of times already, as if she sensed trouble.

His mood darkened even more. He didn't want to involve himself in another's problems, and it was obvious the woman was worried about something.

Suicide? A lovers' meeting? Some clandestine plan that he couldn't begin to imagine? The scenarios raced through his mind. He had a gut feeling that nothing good would come of this encounter.

It never paid to give in to desperation, Alison Harvey reminded herself sternly. She was tired. She was hungry. And she might also be lost.

No. She wasn't lost. She had only to follow the faint trail back to the place where the little stream cut across it, then down the stream to her car hidden behind some trees in a rocky clearing off the gravel road.

For some reason she'd thought this would be easy. Finding her sister when she obviously didn't want to be found was proving difficult and exasperating. Janis had told her, on one of her infrequent calls, that she was visiting friends at a ranch in this area.

"Not to worry," the younger sibling had said with her usual disregard of any but her own desires.

One of the advantages to managing her father's local senate office was that one learned how to get in-

formation. Alison had checked the county records for
the location of the ranch where her sister was staying.
Getting there without local knowledge was another
story.

Spying a sturdy boulder close by, she perched on
it and removed her hiking shoe. After shaking out the
tiny pebble that had embedded itself in her sock under
her right heel, she replaced the shoe, took a drink,
eyed the water left in the bottle and decided that
maybe she should go to plan B.

Too bad she didn't have one.

Find her sister and get her home. That was her
goal—and her promise to her mother—and why she
was running around in the hills like some modern-day
Annie Oakley, only without the gun. However, she
did have a can of pepper spray in case she ran into a
bear.

She managed a weak smile at the thought of facing
down a black bear, or worse, a grizzly. On the other
hand, she was adept at handling irate constituents,
politicians and lobbyists. A bear might be a piece of
cake compared to some of those people.

Spotting movement along the sharp bend in the trail
below her, she stiffened and stared intently.

Nothing moved.

She was pretty sure she'd seen something. Perhaps
it had been a deer moving through the brush. Or a
bear.

Ha-ha, she cynically responded to the suggestion
of lurking danger. She hadn't seen a living thing since

she'd started out…was it only that morning? It seemed she'd been hiking for days rather than hours.

Checking her watch, she saw today was still Wednesday, the fifteenth of May. She wondered if the ides of May would be as dangerous for her as the ides of March had been for Julius Caesar. Very funny. She forced her mind past the morbid thought.

It was getting late. Time to be heading back to the Lost Valley B&B where she'd checked in last night. She'd taken longer than she'd intended, but who was to know the road would end at a creek filled with boulders bigger than the tires on her car?

The map from the forestry station showed a road going all the way to the private ranch—resort—whatever the place was where Janis was visiting. So much for accuracy.

The comforting bulge of the cell phone in her jacket pocket reassured her. Apparently there was no telephone at the ranch or anywhere else in this back-of-beyond wilderness. With the cell phone, she remained connected to civilization, even if only in a technological way.

A wave of loneliness washed over her. It was a rare feeling, brought on by the very real isolation of these mountains. She folded her arms across her waist as if to protect herself from danger and her own emotions. She wasn't a despairing type of person. Really, she wasn't.

On the western side of the Seven Devils Mountain range was Hells Canyon, a 5,500-foot trench cut into

the rocky terrain by the Snake River and described as
"one hell after another" by a long-ago mountain
man.

Most of the roads in the area were shown as dotted
lines on the map, meaning they were dirt tracks and
one needed four-wheel-drive vehicles to navigate
them.

Ha. A horse would have a hard time in this place.

She should get back to her car before dark, but
what if she was close to the ranch house?

It could be over the next ridge and all her time
would be wasted if she gave up now. Besides, she'd
just have to do it all over tomorrow. But with food.
Ignoring her grumbling stomach, she pushed on.

Only to the top of the ridge, she reminded the part
of her that didn't want to give up. If she didn't see
anything that looked like a ranch from there, she was
definitely heading down the mountain for the night.

Giving vent to frustration and other emotions in a
heavy sigh, she put her misgivings aside. As she
stood, she again noticed something out of the corner
of her eye. She hesitated, then went on up the trail.
Approaching a tree at a bend in the path, she made a
plan.

After rounding the turn, she stepped to the side and
out of sight. Pressing her shoulder against the trunk
of a mountain maple, she peered through the new
spring leaves on the lower branches.

Nothing.

From this vantage point, she got a glimpse of Lost

Valley and the tiny town of the same name tucked in close to the reservoir. The valley was five thousand feet above sea level. He-Devil Mountain to the north was listed as 9,393 feet in elevation on the map. She was someplace between the two and still climbing. Between the devil and the deep blue sky? She managed a silent laugh at her thoughts.

A shiver chased down her back. The day was warm, in the sixties, but nights were cold in the mountains. Could a person freeze overnight? Refusing to give in to ridiculous fears, she trudged onward and upward.

At last she came to the ridge. Intense disappointment hit her. No road. No fences. No ranch house to welcome the chance visitor with its friendly, twinkling lights. Nothing but trees and more peaks as far as the eye could see.

Where were those dashing cowboys when a damsel needed rescuing?

Ah, well. Defeating the oddest urge to sit down and cry her heart out, she pivoted for the return trip.

As she turned, she spotted something moving through the trees that partially blocked the path from view. She'd been right. There was someone on the trail.

A man in green cammies, looking like a soldier on jungle patrol, paused and bent forward to study the trail.

She watched intently, then realized he was probably looking at her footprints. Her heart seized up.

Don't be silly, she sternly advised her imagination. He wasn't following her. Dressed as he was in camouflage clothing and with a gun slung over his shoulder, he was most likely a hunter. After all, mad murderers didn't search for victims in a forest.

But what if he had followed her from town and was toying with her until he decided to finish...

No, surely she was being melodramatic.

Calming down, she stepped off the trail, then watched as he proceeded. He appeared to be around her age, which was twenty-eight, and had a clean-cut, all-American look in spite of his outfit. His hair was short under his billed cap. He had a firm jaw and a decisive way of moving. She detected a strong sense of purpose in him.

She didn't really feel in any danger—she'd never had any reason to be scared of people and it wasn't in her nature to be a coward—however, she wasn't ignorant of the bad people in the world.

What she really needed at the present was that elusive plan B. Should she stay hidden until he went on up the trail, then follow him? Should she wait for him on the path and ask if he happened to be going to the ranch?

Hide, then head back to the car, she decided. That was the safest course.

She'd make inquiries in town tomorrow, then start out fresh when she knew more about where she was going. She slipped deeper into a willow thicket behind some fir trees and crouched down to wait.

The minutes ticked off. One, two…five, six…nine, then ten…

Where was the man? Had he passed by so silently she hadn't heard one crackle of a twig under his foot?

She didn't dare look. Since movement had caught her attention, she was astute enough to know it would catch his.

A chill swept over her. She felt danger now. Like a bunny sitting as still as possible but knowing the predator was near—

"How long are you planning on sitting there?" A male voice spoke behind her with more than a little exasperation.

"Aaaiii." She leaped to her feet, spun around and shrieked all at the same time, surprising herself as well as him. She was not usually a screamer.

"Be quiet," he ordered.

"You startled me, sneaking up behind me like that." She flashed him a chiding glance to show she was not intimidated by a strange man silently walking up on her in an isolated mountain setting. The fact that he hadn't grabbed her or made any threatening move with the gun helped.

Her heart gave a funny lurch. He was good-looking. *Really* good-looking. His hair was dark, his eyes the bluest she'd ever seen. He stood a couple of inches over six feet and had brawny shoulders, sinewy arms—revealed by shirtsleeves rolled up nearly to his elbows—and a stare like honed steel.

"Who are you?" he asked at the same time she did.

In the silence, they watched each other warily. Alison was aware of the pulsing of blood through her body, of the quiet of the forest, of the loneliness that had assailed her earlier and was now made sharper by another's presence.

"I asked first," he informed her, a frown indenting a crease between his black eyebrows.

She shook her head. "I did."

He cocked his head slightly to one side as he studied her through narrowed eyes as if assessing her mental and physical abilities. "I could find out," he said softly, a threat veiled in the smooth velvet baritone.

Worry and fatigue dissolved into the sharp relief of anger. She'd learned long ago not to be intimidated by bullies or irate citizens. *Don't be a victim* was the first rule of self-defense. "I think not."

Those midnight-blue eyes sized her up. To her surprise, he smiled. It didn't brighten his eyes, it didn't come from the heart, but it was a reprieve from the frown.

"You're right. Uncle Nick doesn't allow us boys to rough up girls."

She recognized a wry resignation in his tone. He didn't want to fool with her, but he'd been raised to be a responsible person. She relaxed and even managed a true smile. "Uncle Nick is a wise man."

"But I do need to see an ID," he added with a hardening of his lean features.

His teeth were very white against the tan of his face, his lips thin but expressive. His eyes were deep-set, causing intriguing shadows that obscured his thoughts. There was a seriousness about him that was reassuring. There was also anger. She supposed she'd interrupted his plans, whatever they might be.

She considered. Her purpose in being there was supposed to be a secret. A politician's career could be ruined by hints of health problems. "I'm just a tourist."

He flicked her a glance that would have cut through stainless steel. "Name?"

"Alison…" No one would believe a last name like Smith or Jones. "Alison," she repeated firmly, determined not to give away more than she had to. "And you?" she challenged, directing the inquisition to him.

He fished out his wallet and flashed an ID at her. It was imprinted with the sheriff's department decal.

"Travis E. Dalton," she read aloud. Dalton was a well-known name in the state's history, first family and all that. "You're a lawman?"

"Volunteer deputy." He put the wallet away. "What are you doing here?"

She decided the truth was the only way. "Looking for someone. My sister," she added at his skeptical stare. "She's needed at home. A family crisis."

"She's in the mountains?"

"She's supposed to be visiting some ranch near here. I didn't realize the road would be impassable."

"What road?" the man asked, showing the first sign of real amusement and more than a hint of irony.

She smiled and relaxed somewhat. A person with a sense of humor couldn't be all bad.

"Put your bear spray away," he advised, "and we'll try to figure out what to do with you. There's a storm coming."

She glanced at the can of pepper stray she'd gotten out just in case she needed protection and slipped it back on her belt loop, then surveyed the clear blue sky.

"What storm?" she asked in the same tone he'd used about the road.

"It'll be here long before you can get back to…" His voice trailed off in question.

"Lost Valley B&B. My car is on the other side of the creek. Where the road ended."

He nodded. "People used to be able to ford there, but some boulders got washed down in the spring thaw." He frowned again and looked resigned to a fate worse than death. "It'll be dark before you get down the trail. Too dangerous. You'll have to stay at my camp."

"That's perfectly all right. I'm sure—"

"You'll stay put until I say it's safe to go down," he interrupted. "Besides, you might be under arrest."

"Arrest! Whatever for?"

"Vagrancy." He gestured toward the pepper spray.

"Pulling a weapon on an officer of the law. Resisting arrest. Lying under interrogation. Pick one."

"What part do you consider lying?" she asked, curious.

"The part you're leaving out. There's no active ranch near here. Why is your sister up here in the wilderness?"

She considered how much to tell the man. Her mother had sworn her to secrecy, and a deputy, even a volunteer one, might make the connection to the senator's family. If her impetuous sister had gotten herself into trouble, there could be a scandal. That put her between a rock and a hard place, so to speak.

"Let's go," he said impatiently.

"Mr. Dalton—" She began and stopped, not at all pleased with the uncertainty she felt.

"Travis," he said curtly.

"Travis," she repeated. She surveyed the deepening shadows, considered the situation and admitted she was probably being foolish to even hesitate. "I accept your kind invitation of hospitality," she said in a light manner, although the urge to weep surrounded her like a persistent swarm of gnats.

She was simply tired and worried about her sister. Her father had revealed his goals recently. He intended to run for governor of the state and wanted his family's support for his ambitions. If he became governor, Alison suspected he would run for president next. She'd been delegated to bring her sister back into the fold.

More seriously, her mother had told her that her father had a small tumor at the base of his skull. He'd refused to have it removed until his other daughter was home, safe and sound. That was the real reason Alison was here in the woods. Her father might have cancer. He needed his family with him. Besides, Janis was his favorite. She could always make him laugh.

Lengthening her stride, she hurried to keep up with the part-time lawman, who had apparently taken her into protective custody or something like that.

Dalton was an old pioneer name. Was he from that hardy stock who had come West after the Civil War? Another branch had been outlaws, she recalled, a murderous gang from the Wild West days of long ago. Her spirits dipped again.

Over an hour later, her guide stopped. Alison blinked in surprise when she realized they had arrived at a camp that was remarkably well hidden.

A tent was placed to advantage under some pine trees. Splotched with green and tan and nearly covered by cleverly placed branches, it blended perfectly with the trees and brush and was almost impossible to see.

She saw no fire ring of stones and wondered if he cooked anything or ate only cold food. Her stomach growled at the thought of dinner.

"Sit," he ordered.

Like a well-trained pet, she did.

Perched on the boulder he pointed out, she glanced at her watch. After seven. The sun had dipped behind the hills west of them. She realized that while some light might linger until nine o'clock, the high peaks cast deep shadows into their area long before that.

"You were right," she told him. "I wouldn't have made it back to my car before nightfall."

His answer was an affirmative grunt as he busied himself about the site. First he let a bag down to the ground from high overhead. It had been suspended from a tree branch higher than any bear or other animal could have reached. The bag was also in camouflage green. The cord that held it was black. She hadn't noticed either one when she'd looked around.

"Here," he said after rummaging around in the bag. He handed her half an apple and half of a square of cheese, keeping the other halves for himself after cutting them with one of those multipurpose knives loved by men.

Murmuring thanks, she downed her share.

He removed dried pouches of food and a can of coffee from the pack. From another hidden cache, he retrieved a tiny stove, along with stacked pans, and started water from the nearby creek to boiling. She wondered if this was the creek that led to the ford and her car. And how long it would take her to follow it there.

"Don't even think about trying to make it," he said as if reading her mind.

She flushed guiltily. "How did you know what I was thinking?"

"Prisoners always think alike."

"I am not a prisoner," she informed him. "I'm familiar with the law. You have no grounds to hold me."

He looked up from his tasks with a stare that froze the blood in her veins. She had never realized how revealing eyes could be, and what she saw was neither kind nor friendly. His show of courtesy was a facade.

He blinked and the dark mood—anger? resentment?—disappeared, leaving a stern, expressionless mask in its wake. That she wasn't welcome in his camp became clear, but he was determined to do his duty by her.

She sighed. Duty was something she understood.

While he finished cooking their meal, she sat in wary silence, misery slicing hot and quick inside her, bringing on that odd need to weep.

Her host was handsome and competent. There was something solid and definite about him. They were alone in a wilderness. For all she knew, they might never get out. She wished they could be friends.

Ah, well, that wasn't in the cards. Her mission was to hunt down her errant sister. Recalling her parents' ambitions, she felt a cage closing about her as she thought of the future and their political plans. Her mother had said they were depending on her. And she always came through. She had to.

Breathing deeply of the rapidly cooling mountain air, she experienced an odd, painful impulse to run and keep running until she reached the point where the earth joined the sky, a place where she could be free—

"Here," he said, breaking into her introspection to hand her a metal plate.

Within thirty minutes of arriving at the camp, they were eating their dinner. He gave her a fork while he used a spoon. She wolfed down as much of the beef and noodle dish as he did. For dessert, he handed her half a candy bar.

"I'm using up your food," she said in apology.

"I'll get more when we go to town tomorrow."

Now that she'd had food, her determination to finish the mission was stronger. Rested and refreshed, in the morning she could surely make it to the ranch. "Uh, I can find my way alone if you'll take me back to the trail I was following."

He shook his head. "I'll have to check out your credentials," he said cryptically.

Just what she needed—every law agency in the state knowing where she was. "Why?"

"I want to know who you are and why you're wandering around in the wilderness on your own."

"Why are you here?" she challenged.

"Business."

"Personal or official?" she retorted.

He hesitated. "Some of both." His glare dared her to question him more. "You were heading deeper into national forestland. Just where is it that you think you're going?"

"The Towbridge ranch."

"Dennis Towbridge has been dead for years. No one lives on his place anymore."

"I'm sure you're mistaken. My sister is visiting friends at their ranch."

He eyed her as if assessing her honesty. "The area is dangerous for a hiker. Local ranchers have had their cattle and sheep butchered recently. They think paramilitarists or squatters have taken up residence in the woods."

A chill settled in her chest. She'd seen reports on the military groups. They could be extremely dangerous, often led by someone with delusions of grandeur. Surely her sister wasn't mixed up with them.

"Is your sister among either group?"

"No. I don't know," she admitted, pulling her jacket over her shoulders as the air cooled.

Her sister had turned twenty-one a few weeks ago. She'd taken off on her own a day later. Their parents were understandably upset.

Janis had another year of college to go, then Father wanted her to work as part of his campaign staff. She was so naturally outgoing, people gravitated toward her charm. She was also something of a free spirit, rebellious when she was thwarted, but usually able to wrap everyone she met around her little finger.

Alison pressed her fingertips over her mouth to stop the disloyal thoughts. She was tired and sometimes it seemed she did everything her family wanted with no concessions for her own wishes and hopes and desires.

However, her father did important work, work she believed in, for the good of the country. She must remember that. Janis was needed at home.

Their father's operation would be carried out in utmost secrecy. If the news was leaked, the press would forever be questioning his health when he announced he was running for president, as she was sure he would.

She sighed at the machinations that formed the core of her existence. Life was very complicated.

Looking at the rugged terrain, breathing the crystal-clear air, she wondered why it had to be. Here in the mountains, things seemed simple. One had to survive, of course, but there was also something more here, something she sensed deep in her heart.

She listened to the quiet. It was peaceful. Yes, that was it. It was peaceful here.

Her host caught her in the act of smiling to herself. When she widened the smile to include him, he frowned and grimly went about the business of cleaning up the dishes.

Obviously he didn't feel the same soulful contentment. Just as obviously, he didn't want to be within a hundred miles of her. Travis Dalton was a recluse and a loner.

She held the smile with an effort and assumed a cheerful manner. Miss Congeniality. Yeah, that was her.

Chapter 2

The temperature grew progressively colder. Alison huddled in her nylon jacket, aware that she'd been ignorant to come into the mountains with so little gear for survival.

Her companion sat silently over his coffee, his face nearly hidden by shadows. She shivered uncontrollably and wished for a cheery fire. There was plenty of dead wood on the ground. Should she suggest it?

"Sorry," he said mysteriously.

He went to the tent and returned with a down parka, also in cammie green, and tossed it to her. She put it on after she saw he had a sweater and a jacket. Snuggled into the fluffy parka, her hands in the pockets, she felt his gaze on her.

"I'm really sorry to be a pest," she said. "It was

stupid to head into the unknown with so little preparation. I assure you I'm not usually like this. It was just…''

"A family crisis," he supplied.

"Yes."

"Do you have some ID on you?"

After handing over her driver's license, she waited tensely for his next pronouncement.

"Alison Harvey. You were born the same year I was." He studied her for a sec as if to judge whether he agreed with the information. His eyes narrowed. "Harvey, as in the esteemed U.S. senator from Idaho?"

"A—a relative," she admitted, hoping he wouldn't catch the hesitation as she replied truthfully but evasively.

He shrugged and handed the ID back. "Your sister may be mixed up with a bad bunch."

"I'm sure it's a mistake. Janis would never do anything illegal." She mentally crossed her fingers, suddenly not sure at all.

This trip, the long day, the man's unrelenting gaze, as if he could sort truth from lies with just a glance, wore on her. It struck her as absurd, being out in a wilderness looking for her prodigal sister. But someone had to do it. If not her, then who?

No one else came to mind, a depressing realization. It always seemed to be her job to smooth out problems in the family. For a second, she felt trapped by that expectation, then she pushed the odd thought aside.

"Why the secrecy?"

"I don't know what you mean," she said coolly, putting on a polite mask that revealed nothing.

"You didn't want me to know who you were."

She tensed. While he didn't give much away about himself, he seemed to be unusually perceptive where she was concerned. She should have had a plan, except she hadn't expected to meet up with a handsome volunteer deputy out in the middle of nowhere.

Candor was often disarming. She decided to try it. "My family doesn't want anyone to know we're looking for my sister. It, uh, might sound as if there's a problem when there isn't. There *is* a complication."

"Such as?"

Could she trust him with the truth? People were wary when it came to illness and the presidency. Not that her father was going to die, but still… "My father has a slight medical situation."

"What kind of situation?"

Alison glared at her inquisitor. "He has a small tumor at the base of his skull. Father doesn't want anyone to know. Like so many men, he thinks illness of any kind is a weakness. My mother told me, and asked that I bring Janis home for the surgery. I promised that I would."

There was a subtle difference in the man's expression. She thought she saw sympathy, perhaps sadness, flash through his eyes. This gave her an inordinate sense of hope that she was doing the right thing.

"I see," he said in a musing tone. "That's tough."

Alison nodded. "So you see, I have to make it to the ranch and talk to Janis. She'll come home once I explain things to her."

"Put a guilt trip on her," the man corrected. "The same as your mother did to you." He shook his head. "Sending an inexperienced female into the mountains. That was smart."

The forlorn hope went up in a puff of smoke. She didn't need his approval anyway. Clenching her hands in the warm jacket pockets, she didn't bother to respond. She'd learned that was the best way to handle remarks about her family.

Travis noted the way Alison clammed up at any criticism of her family. She was protective of them.

Brave, too, to venture into the hills like this, he grudgingly admitted, but ignorant of the dangers. However, neither her courage nor her family loyalty meant a flaming thing to him, other than the nuisance factor.

At nine, he suggested it was time to go to bed. That visibly got her attention. She sat up straight and stared at him. "Where shall I sleep?"

"In the tent."

"Where will you be?"

He spoke slowly and patiently. "It's a two-man, uh, -person, tent. There are two sleeping bags. Sometimes it gets chilly—or I meet up with a lost hiker."

"Oh." She took a minute to consider, then nodded. As if they had any other choice.

He heated water in a pan. "You can wash up behind those bushes over there. Toss the water on the ground, not into the creek. Don't stray off."

She rose and looked around, then headed toward the thicket across the slope from the camp. While she prepared for bed, he closed the bear bag and pulled it high into the air, the nylon cord suspended over a tree branch at least twenty feet from the ground.

Bears were getting smarter, he mused while he waited for his guest to reappear. Some of them had learned they only needed to follow the rope to its end, break it and food would fall to the ground like manna from heaven. He used a black rope, which was harder to see, and ran it through some brush to further disguise it, then secured it to a tree.

Glancing at the luminous dial of his watch, he decided she'd had enough time. He rose and strode toward the bushes. "Yo," he called out. "About finished?"

"Yes," she said, returning to camp.

The relief surprised him. He'd half expected her to try to escape in the dark. She was smarter than that, thank heavens. There were other things he'd noticed about her. The fact that she was putting up a cheerful front was one.

Her lips, a soft pink without lipstick, had trembled ever so slightly at times. When she thought he wasn't looking, the despair returned. In spite of the smiles, he detected a delicate vulnerability in the smoky-green eyes.

It wasn't a fact he wanted to know. He didn't give a damn what her problems were. He closed his eyes for a second. Couldn't a man just be left alone?

Leaning on the anger that had gotten him through the blackest days of his life, he grabbed his kit, brushed his teeth and prepared for bed. After that, he stored the stove and pans in their bag and pulled them back into the air.

Slowly, reluctantly, he went to the tent. It would be tight quarters in there. He hadn't been that close to a woman in two years.

Women had tried to comfort him, but he hadn't wanted them. He hadn't wanted the passion. Passion brought memories and memories brought pain. He willed the abyss into stillness as he opened the nylon flap and ducked inside.

She was tucked safely in one of the down bags, her back to him. Her hair was a pool of shadowy waves against the material. He knew it would be warm if he ran his fingers into it. And in the sunlight, it gleamed like gold.

A spasm rippled through him, a strong, undefined emotion that took him by surprise. Odder still was the fatalistic notion that he wouldn't make it through the night if he slept in here.

He considered taking his down bag outside and sleeping under a tree, but the temperature was dropping fast.

Don't be stupid, he ordered. He could handle one night. It wasn't as if it meant anything. Nothing had impinged on his heart or his soul for a long time. Nothing ever would again, if he had any say about it.

After removing his shoes, he stored them under the rain fly, zipped the door flap and scooted into the sleeping bag.

A spark shot up his leg as his foot brushed against hers, causing heat to spear through his gut. Memories, too painful to bear, stirred at the accidental touch.

Two years ago, he'd been awakened by his wife's moans. She'd been in labor. He'd gotten her to the hospital, but it had been too late, too late for Julie and too late for their unborn son. With all the modern miracles of medicine, the doctors hadn't been able to revive that which was gone.

"Don't grieve," she'd said during that grim trip to town that had ended in hell for him. "I'll love you forever. I'll always be with you."

Julie, ever the optimist. For them, forever had been their three years of marriage. She'd died that night.

He willed the memory and the agony into the pit of oblivion where he'd consigned all his dreams and hopes.

Finally he was able to see a certain irony in the present situation. Not wanting to be close to anyone, here he was, sleeping with a woman, one who was a relative of the state's most popular senator.

Wait a minute. The senator had two daughters. The older one worked in his Boise office. He recalled seeing her on television a couple of times, always discreetly in the background when her father was announcing his campaign for office or making a statement to the press.

This woman had to be one and the same. She was prettier and more approachable than he'd thought. Up close, there was something valiant about her, but also something fragile. She'd been ethereal standing in the pool of sunlight on the trail, as if only her will kept her pinned to earth.

He cursed silently, not wanting to know these things about her. *Live and let live;* that was his motto.

Pushing the sleeping bag down to his waist, he put his arms behind his head for a pillow and stared into the darkness of the tent. From over the near peaks, he heard the rumble of a building storm. He doubted it would rain much, so they should get out without difficulty tomorrow.

Alison stirred and turned toward him, snuggling her nose into his armpit. A bolt of hunger went through him like summer lightning.

Stunned and rock-hard with needs he didn't want, he thought this chance encounter with the senator's daughter just might be the death of him. He hoped it came soon.

She moved closer. Her hair tickled his chin. He smoothed it down, unable to stop his fingers from running through its softness. It was like warm, spun gold.

He tensed for the pain he knew would follow.

Instead, an odd sensation, like the gentle caress of a breeze, flowed over him. He thought of things he'd left behind years ago—the comforting touch of his mother as she tucked him into bed, his father's rough but careful hands as he lifted him high off the ground, gave him a mighty toss, then caught him, the older man's laughter blending with his shouts of glee. Later, there had been Julie, his friend, his lover, his beloved. That's what happiness had been. Once.

Old wounds ripped open. He held on until the old dreams faded. He would never allow himself to be that vulnerable again. It wasn't a vow, only a certainty embedded in the granite that enclosed his heart.

Turning his back on the sleeping woman, he welcomed the darkness.

Alison woke with a groan. Her companion pushed the sleeping bag aside. She realized it had been his stirring that had awakened her.

"The ground makes for a hard mattress," he said. "Even with pine straw under the tent."

"I noticed." She peered at the faint light in the clearing through the mosquito net. "What time is it?"

"Time to get going. Around five," he added when she frowned at him. "I want to get to town before noon."

"Why?"

"So I can get back before dark."

It came to her that he would rather walk across burning coals than have to deal with her. So much for femme fatale. "You wouldn't be going to town if it weren't for me."

"True."

"So, take me back to the trail."

"No."

The flat refusal told her he would do his duty as he saw it no matter what she wanted. She was silent while he put on his shoes, then left the tent. Combing her fingers through her hair, she watched him let down the bear bag and start water to boiling.

"Coffee?" he called.

"Please."

"You take anything in it?"

"Nothing, thanks." She cautiously pushed the covers down, hating to leave the coziness of the sleeping bag for the great outdoors, which was decidedly cold.

"Stay put. I'll bring it to you."

To her amazement, he did just that. While she sipped the wonderfully warm brew, he fried bacon, prepared scrambled eggs and toasted bread slices on a fork. Again he told her to sit still and served her in the tent.

"I thought campers weren't supposed to have food in their sleeping quarters."

"That's right. I'm making an exception for you."

"Why?"

"It's about thirty-six degrees this morning," he told her. "I don't want you taking a chill before I get you off the mountain. My camp doesn't extend to nursing facilities.''

Grim Reality 101. He was truthful if nothing else.

Watching him while she ate, she decided he might act contrary, he might not want to deal with her, but he was really very nurturing, even though he didn't like her for some reason. She refused to let herself be hurt by this insight.

After eating, she set her plate outside, donned her hiking boots, then joined him in the clearing, the warm parka fastened up to her neck. She handed her plate and fork over when he held out a soapy hand. In a few minutes, he had the bags stored in the air again.

''Ready?''

She nodded, touching her hair self-consciously when she saw his glance on it. Her comb was in her purse, which was in the trunk of her car. She'd only carried her wallet and cell phone with her.

He turned abruptly and headed down the mountain via a different route from the one she'd hiked yesterday. She followed silently, aware of the wall of dislike he'd erected between them.

In much less time than it had taken her to go up the mountain yesterday, they arrived at the creek ford. He went at once to her car as if he'd parked it himself.

''How did you know my car was here?''

He waited while she dug her keys out of her jeans pocket. ''I saw the sunlight glinting off the bumper.''

Once she was inside, he leaned down to her window. "I'll follow you into town."

"On foot?"

"In my truck."

To her astonishment, he disappeared behind some brush, tossed a bush aside, then backed a pickup into the clearing. She hadn't seen his vehicle at all.

At his gesture, she started her midsize luxury sedan, a graduation present from her parents six years ago. Where had the time gone? Where had her dreams gone?

She headed down the bumpy road to the county highway. An hour later, they passed the small lake formed by a dam and arrived in Lost Valley, a bustling community that served the ranchers and tourists who drove through the valley on their way to Yellowstone or Hells Canyon in the summer.

In the winter, she imagined the place must go into hibernation. The snow would be deep at five thousand feet and last all season. She shivered, imagining it.

Parking at the Lost Valley B&B, she mused on what it would be like, being snowed in for days. Her gaze was drawn to Travis as they stood on the gravel parking apron in front of the old Victorian house.

"Stay out of the woods," he advised without preamble. "I'll look for your sister. Are you going home?"

"I'll stay. I have to talk to Janis." She retrieved her purse from the trunk of the car.

He nodded. His thick black hair blew across his

forehead in attractive disarray. For some reason, she thought of the crisp, woodsy scent that had surrounded her like a warm cocoon during the night. She realized it had come from him.

"I'll bring her to town." He gazed down the street. "I'll have to tell the sheriff that you two are in the area. Don't worry. He can keep a secret."

At his sardonic tone, her whole endeavor suddenly seemed foolish. Stiffly, she thanked him for his help. When he returned to his truck, she called, "Mr. Dalton...Travis. Don't tell Janis why I'm here. Please."

He nodded, then climbed into the pickup and left.

Alison went inside. Amelia Miller, the amiable owner of the place, greeted her. "Are you okay? I was worried when I didn't see you come in last night. Not that I keep tabs on my guests, but..." Her voice trailed off. "Well, anyway, I'm glad you made it back."

"I'm fine. I was hiking and it got late."

Amelia nodded. "So you spent the night at the Dalton place," she concluded. "I saw Travis outside with you. I didn't realize you had friends here."

Alison debated about telling the truth. She hated to lie, but neither did she feel like explaining. "More like acquaintances," she said.

Amelia's gray eyes took on a speculative aspect. "All the girls in town have been in love with one of the Daltons at some point in their lives. Some people say Seven Devils Mountains were named after the

Dalton bunch, but there're only five boys. And one girl.''

''Plus Uncle Nick,'' Alison added, recalling the name.

''Yes, that does make seven, doesn't it? I understand the uncle and his two brothers—they were also twins—were hellions in their younger days, too.''

''Too?'' Alison asked. She defended her interest in the Daltons as natural after her encounter.

''Travis and his twin, Trevor, were pretty wild in school, not mean or dangerous, but fun and totally fearless. All the Daltons are known for their courage.'' She mentioned others in the family, including a doctor, lawyer and deputy sheriff. ''The youngest cousin is the girl,'' Amelia finished.

Alison's mind reeled. Twins. Brothers. Cousins. So many Daltons. If they were anything like Travis, meeting them would be daunting.

She rushed up the broad, curving staircase before Amelia could ask her anything about the Dalton family and she had to confess she knew nothing of them.

In her room she locked the door, then took a shower and changed to fresh slacks and a knit top. She hesitated, then picked up the phone and dialed her mother's personal number. The older woman answered right away.

''Mother, it's Alison.''

''Oh, good. Do you have any news of Janis?''

For the briefest instant, Alison wondered why her mother couldn't have asked after her health first.

However, no one knew of her strange night, so it was unfair to expect concern where there was no cause.

"Not yet. I'm still looking. The ranch she told me about is in a remote location. The road is washed out, so I'll have to hike in."

"How long do you think it will take?"

Alison heard the anxiety in her mother's voice. "I'm not sure. A couple of days, I should think. I'll hurry, but the mountain trail is steep and rough."

"Thank you, darling. I know you'll find Janis and convince her to come home at once."

Alison wished she felt as certain. "How's Father?"

"Oh, you know him. Stubborn as ever." Her mother lowered her voice. "He refuses to even consider surgery at present."

Until the beloved but prodigal daughter was back in the fold, Alison interpreted. "I'll do the best I can."

"Of course," her mother said.

After they hung up, Alison sat in the white wicker chair and contemplated her life. A smile tugged at her lips as she thought about Travis Dalton and his wild relatives. It would have been fun to grow up with them, to have known them when she was young.

Twenty-eight wasn't *that* old. However, at times she did feel ancient. Seven years older than her sibling, it seemed she'd always had to baby-sit while her parents went to political and social functions. She'd felt responsible for Janis and her behavior.

She wondered why.

It was such an odd thought she forgot to dry her hair as she sat and tried to figure out why the last two days seemed so momentous, as if she'd gone through one of those life-changing epiphanies she'd read about.

Funny.

"Hey, bro," Trevor yelled across the street.

Travis swung around to face his twin. He cursed. Trevor could be a pain. He waited for the other to cross the busy street and catch up with him.

"Where you headed?" Trevor wanted to know, falling into step with him.

"The cafe."

"Great. You can treat your favorite brother to lunch just to show everyone what a good guy you are," Trevor said.

"They already know I'm a good guy. It's you who are questionable."

"Yeah, but what about that blonde I saw you talking to over at the B&B?" Trevor poked him in the ribs with an elbow.

"Business," was his terse reply.

"Right," Trevor declared, his blue eyes alight with mischief. "I like that kind of business. So she helped out while you were digging for gold up in the woods?"

Travis gave his twin a warning glance. He was in no mood for nonsense this morning. "How the hell do you know about that?"

"I saw you on the highway and followed when I realized you were following another car. Who is she?"

Travis entered the café, his brother hot on his heels. He chose a table where he could see the street in the direction of the B&B where he'd left Alison two hours ago. He needed to eat, pick up supplies and head back to the hills. After a restless night, he wanted the solitude.

"How's Uncle Nick?" he asked after they'd ordered.

"Mean as a snake and twice as ugly," Trevor said. "You better plan on being home for his birthday or the old boy will come after you with his six-shooter."

"I'll be there."

Their uncle had taken in the whole brood of Daltons after the deaths of his two brothers twenty-two years ago. That the cousins would do anything in the world for him was a given.

"Bring the blonde," Trevor suggested. "What did you say her name was?"

"I didn't."

The twins flashed identical smiles, one guarded, the other devilish.

"I'll find out," Trevor promised.

"Leave her alone," Travis said in a serious tone. "She's looking for someone."

Trevor was immediately intrigued. "Who?"

"Her sister, she says." He shrugged to indicate he didn't know if that was true or not.

"You mean there's another like her?" His twin

waggled his eyebrows. "Hey, this is sounding more interesting. Where did you meet her?"

"In the woods."

That piqued his twin's curiosity, but Travis wouldn't tell him another thing. After making Trev chip in his share of the meal, he left his sibling devising various ways to meet the stranger and her sister. Travis wondered if he should warn Alison about his devil-may-care bro, then decided she could watch out for herself.

Another complication had arisen. The sheriff had suggested using her as bait to infiltrate the group, either squatters or paramilitarists, up in the hills, assuming her sister was mixed up with them. After he'd explained the probable connection to the senator, both had agreed it was wiser to get the two women out of the area ASAP.

Sunlight glinted off mica in the sidewalk outside the window, little sparkles of brilliance that reminded him of the woman he'd found in the woods.

A sensation like the heat lightning that had zigzagged across the night sky ran over him. Alison Harvey had opened a door inside him that he wanted to stay closed.

Grimly he reviewed the unexpected passion. He didn't want hunger or need. He didn't want involvement of any kind. He simply wanted to be left alone.

Was that too much to ask?

He would bring her sister to town so the two of them could leave. Then he'd head back to the mine and the solitude he craved. End of episode.

Chapter 3

Alison handed over her credit card. The clerk didn't notice the name or make any connection to her family. She signed the credit slip and eyed her purchases.

"I'll make two trips," she said.

The teenager behind the counter gave her a cheery smile. "I'll help."

Living in a small town had its advantages. No one in the city would have considered leaving the store to help a person carry her shopping bags to the car. Of course, the environment was different there, not so trusting.

The young man hoisted the backpack onto one shoulder, then grabbed two bags. She picked up the last one and directed him to her vehicle. They stored the items in the back seat. Before she could decide whether to tip him or not, he gave her a friendly salute and headed back into the sporting-goods store.

She tossed her purse into the car, intending to head to the B&B, sort through her purchases and pack for the trip. Just then, she spotted a familiar figure coming toward her.

With his masculine physique, dark hair and startling blue eyes, wearing a cowboy hat pushed back on his forehead, tight jeans and a chambray shirt, he looked the archetypal cowboy, at home in this rugged country.

Her heart clenched into a knot that swelled until it crowded her lungs to the point where she couldn't breathe. There was something about Travis Dalton that unraveled her usual composure.

She waited warily, then was surprised at his smile—a real smile, relaxed and pleasant and cheery. She glanced away, feeling unsure and sort of achy inside. This wasn't good, not at all. She met his eyes when he stopped.

"Hi, there," he said. "I'm not Travis."

She sorted through the greeting and came to a logical conclusion. "Then you must be the twin."

"Right. I'm Trevor, the handsome, friendly one. Travis is the ugly, mean twin. I'm also older by twenty minutes…in case you like older men." He tipped his hat to her.

Her heart eased. "I'm glad to meet you."

"I saw you at Amelia's place with Travis this morning."

"I'm staying there." She noted the speculation in his eyes. Did he know she'd spent the night in the mountains with his twin?

He eyed the sporting-goods store, her purchases so clearly visible in the car, then her. "You going on a backpacking trip?"

"No," she said quickly.

He looked skeptical.

"Not exactly," she amended. She considered, then, figuring he'd learn the facts from his twin, decided to take him into her confidence. "Actually, I'm looking for someone. My sister is visiting a ranch north of here, near He-Devil Mountain. The Towbridge place. Perhaps you could direct me on getting there?"

"You don't want to go up there," Trevor said, his expression becoming dead serious. "It could be dangerous, especially for a lone hiker."

"Travis warned me of the paramilitary gang and the squatters. I intend to avoid them. Is there a road to the ranch house, perhaps from the northern approach?"

Trevor shook his head. "Only one way in and that's by an old gravel road. It may not be passable."

"It isn't. The ford has boulders washed across it. A car can't make it." She sighed and gave him her best big-eyed, helpless look, something she despised when other women used it. Desperate times called for desperate measures. She had come up with an idea. "Is there a guide I could hire? With horses, it should be an easy trip."

She hoped he would volunteer.

"Not around here. You'll have to go to Council. That's the county seat. But I doubt the fishing guides know the mountains well enough to get you in and out safely. Travis is your best bet. He's prospected all over the hills, looking for gold. Too bad he won't take you," Trevor told her, certainty in his voice.

Curiosity got the better of her. "Why won't he?"

After the briefest hesitation, the brother said, "It's not his thing. He's sort of a loner."

This information wasn't news. Travis had made it clear he was an unwilling rescuer. "Well, thanks for your help."

"Travis isn't going to like it when he hears you're heading out by yourself," Trevor said.

"How will he know?" she challenged.

"Well, I'll have to tell him." His eyes flashed with wicked delight.

"This is really none of your business. Nor your brother's. I have business at the ranch, urgent family business, and no one can stop me from crossing public land to get there."

Trevor snorted at her declaration. "You a lawyer?"

"No."

"Why don't you come out to the ranch and talk to Trav before you take off?" the twin invited. "Uncle Nick would like to meet you."

Alison was wary of the sudden change in subject. "Why would Uncle Nick want to meet me?"

"Well, you spent the night on the mountain with his nephew, for one thing."

"How did you know about that?" she demanded, furious that Travis would tell his family about her foolish trip.

The twin chuckled. Alison realized he'd been fishing for information. And had gotten it.

"I saw him follow you to Amelia's place this morning," he explained smoothly.

"So you decided to hang around and accost me?" she asked with an acid sting in her tone, angry that she'd been tricked into confirming his suspicions. She was better at handling people than that. Usually.

"Sorry. I didn't mean to upset you," Trevor said in a consoling manner.

"I'm not upset." She spoke through gritted teeth.

Her eyes met pure blue ones. His grin was so good-natured and understanding, she couldn't help the smile that sprang to her lips at the blatant lie.

"Come out to the ranch and talk to Travis. He's staying there until tomorrow," Trevor urged. "You can have supper with us. Uncle Nick is a great cook."

Alison shook her head. She wanted nothing more to do with Travis Dalton. He stirred something inside her that she didn't like. Or maybe she liked it too much.

Anyway, he confused her, and she had no time for personal qualms. She had a job to do.

Travis stepped off the porch of the double-winged ranch house that had originally been a log cabin. Trevor had returned with the pickup piled high with bags of feed for the horses. Restless, he went to help unload.

Hefting a fifty-pound bag, Trevor grinned at him as if he had a secret.

"What?" Travis demanded, grabbing another bag.

"I met your girlfriend," his twin said as they entered the storage shed. "The one you spent the night with up on the mountain." He heaved the bag onto the shelf.

Travis didn't fall for the attempt to weasel information out of him. He tossed his bag on top of the other with a grunt. "Yeah? Did she tell you all about it?"

"Uh-huh. She said she was looking for her long-lost sister and ran into you. What I want to know is—did she sleep in your tent alone, or were you there with her?"

For a split second, Travis was dumbfounded... which was just long enough for his brother to know he'd hit upon the truth. Trevor broke into guffaws.

"Okay, so you know the whole story," Travis admitted, feeling defensive. "Keep it quiet, will you?"

"Uncle Nick would find it very interesting that the elusive Travis Dalton holed up in the hills with a woman. A real pretty one," Trevor added. "By the way, she's heading into the hills again."

Travis was sure he'd misunderstood. "What?"

The mischievous light faded from Trevor's eyes,

and he became serious. "It's true. She bought a back-pack and camping gear at the sporting goods store. The owner's son was working the counter. He says she prepared for a long hiking trip with a supply of freeze-dried food packets, plus lots of jerky and choc-olate and coffee."

"That little fool. Somebody needs to pound some sense into her head." It wouldn't be him. He'd warned her about the dangers of the mountains. If she got into trouble this time, it was on her head, not his.

"You probably ought to talk to her," Trevor sug-gested.

"I told her to stay put at Amelia's."

"Well, I don't think she listened. She's definitely heading out, probably at first light."

Travis shrugged and tried not to recall a shimmer-ing spotlight of gold. Or the fragile tremble of soft lips. Or smoky-green eyes filled with despair. "Not my problem."

"She mentioned hiring a guide. Maybe you should take her to her sister if you know where she is."

"The Towbridge ranch." He'd known, watching her through the binoculars, that he should have stuck with his business and left her to hers. He'd known she was going to be trouble with a capital *T*. This merely confirmed it. "Why don't you take her there, since you're so damn concerned?"

Trevor shot him a hard glance. "You're the one who found her. I figure she's your responsibility."

"I don't." A ripple of emotion flowed over the smooth surface of the abyss, stirring the depths he didn't want disturbed. His responsibility? Huh. Let some other fool jump in and be the hero. He wouldn't.

"Man, you have changed," his twin said slowly. "I thought you were okay now, but I guess when you lost your wife, you lost touch with the human race."

"Shut up," he said, no emotion, no heat, just a deadly warning in the two words.

Trevor stuck his chin out. "Make me."

For half a second, Travis considered doing it. Giving vent to the anger inside would be a relief. Temporarily. He went to the truck and holsted another fifty-pounder, Trevor following, his gaze mocking.

"It isn't worth the effort," he said.

Trevor lifted the feed sack to his shoulder. "What is?" he asked softly. "What's worth anything to you these days, little brother?"

The black surface roiled, filling him with hot bitterness that wanted to erupt. He forced it at bay. "Not a thing," he said just as softly. "Not a damn thing."

Silence followed at their heels as they completed their work, then Trevor stalked off without a backward glance.

Travis stood at the paddock and patted an inquisitive mare's neck. Sunlight cast red highlights into the light-brown hide. The mare murmured low in her throat and nudged his hand when he stopped.

He thought of the woman who had snuggled against him, seeking warmth, of soft hair laced with gold, warm under his hand, of courage, foolish as it was, that had kept her going when she trembled with weariness.

Even while he fought with his conscience, he knew he was on the losing end of the rope. A sense of self-preservation urged him to simply call and warn her off, but he went to his pickup and grimly cranked the engine.

His twin was wrong. He hadn't lost all sense of human kindness, but life would be easier if he did.

Alison's car was gone when he pulled up in front of the B&B. Frowning, he went inside. Amelia was on the phone. He waited while she wrote down a reservation, then hung up.

"Travis, hello. What can I do for you?" she asked, obviously curious.

"Uh, I need to see one of your guests."

"Miss Harvey is gone."

"What do you mean—gone?"

"She left this afternoon. She'll be back day after tomorrow. That'll be Saturday. Today is Thursday." Amelia offered the reminder when he didn't say anything.

"I *know* what day it is," he said. Yeah, trouble with a capital *T*. He'd known it from the first glance. "What time did she leave?"

"Midafternoon. Around two. She's visiting relatives in the area. That's what she said," Amelia added defensively.

Travis calculated the time element. Alison had

nearly a three-hour jump on him. It would have taken her at least an hour to get to the creek. From there, she would have to hike. She'd planned for a two-night trip, so maybe she'd stay in her car tonight and take off at first light, figuring an overnight stay when she found her sister, then hiking out Saturday and returning to the B&B.

Satisfied that he understood the plan, he thanked Amelia and left. He'd head Alison off at the ford.

Alison let the backpack slip to the ground. She hadn't done this kind of thing since the last time she'd gone to camp fifteen years ago. Whew, she obviously wasn't in the same shape now as she'd been as a teenager.

She sat on a log and wiped her face before taking a drink of water. Nibbling on trail mix, she rested for ten minutes. While some part of her urged that she hurry, she knew a break every hour or so was a more efficient way of traveling in the mountains.

Leaning against the stump of a tree, she let the quiet run through her like a life-giving stream. Her days were always filled with duties, appointments and crises, it seemed. She never had time to simply relax—

"Where the hell do you think you're going?" a coldly furious male voice interrupted her musings.

Alison jerked around in shock. "You!"

"Yeah. Me. If I'd been a grizz, you would already be dinner."

She tried to quell his temper with sarcasm. "That's rather dramatic, don't you think?"

"I've been thinking a lot the last three and a half hours, mostly about what I'd like to do when I caught up with you. The possibilities were endless."

"I'm glad you were entertained," she said just as coolly. "You needn't have followed. I'm not a teen-ager out past curfew, in case you haven't noticed."

His gaze ran over her so hotly she was surprised she didn't melt on the spot. "Pick up your gear," he ordered. "We're heading back."

She decided humor was the better part of valor. "Sorry, I can't. I have a job to complete. Neither hail, nor snow, nor dark of night, also irate ranchers, prospectors and volunteer deputies, shall stop me from doing it."

"Very funny. You may be interfering with an on-going investigation. I can arrest you for that."

"I'm not, and you can't." She pushed her fingers through her hair in frustration and tilted her head to frown at him. "You bring out the worst in me."

His harsh expression didn't alter. They were silent for a long minute, locked in an impasse. Regret and longing mingled. Sensing the unexplained hostility in him, she watched his eyes for a clue to his next action.

"I told you I'd bring your sister to you," he finally said. "I generally keep my word."

"I don't think she'll come with a stranger." She observed the deepening of the frown line over the bridge of his nose. His eyes were hard and opaque, as if his thoughts had disappeared behind granite.

"Then I'll just have to tie her up and force her off the mountain." He glanced around. "Were you planning on pitching camp or walking all night?"

"I thought I'd follow the stream up to your camp, stay there for the night and start out early in the morning. I brought an alarm clock so I can get up at the crack of dawn." She gave him a bright smile.

"Okay," he said, giving in so easily she was startled and more wary of him than ever. "Let's go."

"Is this some kind of trick?" she asked. "Because if it is, let me remind you that my father wields some power in this state—oh!" She realized she'd given herself away.

"Watch it, the politician's daughter is showing through your meek facade."

So he'd already figured it out. She shrugged. "You'd be surprised at the number of people who fall for that line."

He didn't crack a smile. "Yeah, right. Let's head for camp. It'll be dark within an hour."

This time he put her in front and kept an eye on her the whole way as they followed the stream upward, ever upward, into the Seven Devils Mountains.

"Whoa," he said just as she was beginning to wonder if they were lost.

She looked around and realized she'd nearly walked past the place. If she'd done that while on her own…well, someone would surely have found her before she starved to death wandering around in circles.

"Where shall I pitch my tent?" she asked.

"Wherever you decide," he said in a snarl.

While he let the bear bags slip to the ground, she searched out the best place for her tent. Naturally he'd chosen the perfect spot, a level section with a layer of pine needles for extra padding.

A site near the creek looked inviting. Except she might not hear a bear if it approached her tent during the night due to the burbling of the stream. She explored another on the opposite side of the clearing, but there was a boulder in the middle of it. After a couple of attempts to dislodge it, she gave up.

On the other side of his tent was a nice location. It was rock-free, littered with pine straw…and close to him in case she needed his help during the night.

Several scenarios played out in her mind in quick order, all of them ending with her in *his* tent again.

Cheeks flushed, she extended her search among the adjacent trees. All day, visions of the previous night had run like a continuous film through her head. Travis had been the most thoughtful of hosts, a true gentleman in all ways.

Her heart catapulted around like a jumping bean.

Startled, she pressed a hand to her chest. Of all the men she had ever met, none had given her that sense of…of peace and security she'd experienced with him.

"You having a heart attack or something?" he asked in his usual caustic manner.

"No. I was just trying to decide where to put the tent." She gave him a mock frown. "You have the best place."

He gave an impatient snort. "Put your tent on that level spot right behind mine."

Her heart jumped and beat in her throat. She nodded and took her bundle to the site. Opening the compact bag, she removed the set of hollow plastic sticks with the stretchable cord running through them and put them together the way the teenager had shown her so that they formed one long pole.

There were three of these devices, two going one way and one running opposite, thus forming the supports of the tent. She removed the tent and tried to figure out which flap to run the first support through. She learned that one demonstration did not constitute expertise.

"Lay the tent out flat and square it up," Travis advised. "Then you'll see the shape of it and the guides for the supports." He picked up a pine branch from the ground and returned to his tasks.

Following his directions, she found it was easy to see how the tent worked once it was neatly laid out. She quickly ran the supports through the guides, then inserted each end through a loop. The tent popped upright into a dome shape. She grinned as if she'd won a blue ribbon.

She remembered to stake each side so the wind

wouldn't blow the tent, her in it, down the mountain. Finished, she grabbed the wool sweater and jacket from her pack, then returned to the clearing. Supper bubbled in a pot over the tiny gas stove and a fire crackled in a shallow pit.

"Oh, wonderful," she murmured, sitting on a log that Travis had pulled into position in front of the fire and putting on the outerwear. "Aren't you afraid someone will see the fire and come investigate?"

"No."

She studied his lean face in the leaping shadows created by the fire. "You're angry," she concluded.

"Damn right."

"Why?"

He paused in stirring the pot and directed a cutting stare her way. His eyes were dark in the firelight.

Mysterious. Dangerous. Exciting.

Something ancient and primitive stirred within her. A part of her seemed to have awakened from a deep sleep.

Right. Sleeping Beauty and all that.

"What have I done to earn your animosity?" she asked, determined to get to the root of his problem.

"This isn't a safe place for anyone, man or woman, to be running around alone. A greenhorn like you shouldn't be allowed out without a nanny."

At his scorn, her spirits dropped several notches. "I have to see my sister."

She spoke quietly, convincingly. Travis had to give

her an A for determination. "I said I would bring her to you."

Her eyes were fathoms deep, glowing with rich lights from the reflection of the fire. He had a sudden vision of simply picking her up and taking her to his tent, there to have his way with her the whole night through.

His heart did some strange, painful things. Okay, so there was a sexual attraction. He stared at her hair, the way the firelight shot sparks into it. He forced himself to look away.

"I know. I appreciate that, really I do," she insisted when he glanced at her again. "But I gave my word."

He sensed the struggle inside her as she tried to explain, but he understood perfectly. Like honor and duty, a person's word was sacred. He'd once given his word to cherish and protect, but he'd failed.

With a silent curse, he spurned the memory. The past was gone, and nothing he could ever do would change it.

"Supper," he said more gruffly than he meant.

He held out a plate and fork, ignoring the air of vulnerability that surrounded her slender form as she sat perfectly still for an instant.

Then, "I have my own things," she told him.

She dashed to her backpack and returned with a fork. Smiling brilliantly—as if she'd thought of everything—she took the plate and sat on the log, moving over so he, too, could use it. Not once did she look at him.

Fine. Let her keep her distance. He intended to. But first, he had to get past an odd knot that had formed right under his breastbone as she smiled and ate and murmured over how good the food was.

So her eyes looked sad and uncertain as she hunched over the plate, the delicate line of her head and neck and spine in one gentle curve of hidden anxiety. So what?

He chose to sit on the ground and use the log for a backrest. He stretched his legs out along one side of the fire. In a minute she did the same.

After eating and cleaning their dishes, he made them each a cup of spiced cider from a mix. Slowly a sense of contentment stole over him. It felt so odd he couldn't identify the condition at first.

"It's so peaceful here," she murmured, picking up the thought. "I had no idea. I now understand why people like to get away by going to the wilderness. Life can be such a treadmill at times…"

Her voice trailed into silence. The refined planes of her face took on a pensive mood as she gazed into the fire. When she met his eyes, she seemed troubled, but again she smiled. He was beginning to dislike that fake cheer.

Not that it was his business. Whatever her problems, she would have to work them out, he reminded himself savagely. At the moment, he didn't have a care in the world. He wanted to keep it that way.

He yawned as the fire burnt down to embers. "I'm heading for bed," he told her.

"Me, too."

He secured the campsite, stirring the embers and drowning them completely. After making sure the supply bags were suspended, he recalled her backpack.

"Did you bring any rope?" he asked.

"Yes."

"Get it and we'll hang your pack up in case the local wildlife decides to poach. The ground squirrels have been known to chew a hole right through the material."

He showed her how to tie a rock on the end of the rope, toss it over a high branch, then tie her pack to the line and haul it up into the air.

Her hands on the rope brushed his as they worked together. He was aware of her body and its slender agility, of her determination to show him she could do a good job, of something in her that was soft, as soft as the pale pink lips that trembled ever so slightly at the corners when she didn't keep her guard up.

Hell. He didn't want the awareness. Moving away, he tied the rope around a handy tree trunk.

When she told him good-night and disappeared inside her dome tent, he experienced a return of the more primitive urges that had plagued him since spying her through the binoculars yesterday.

Maybe he was low on the milk of human kindness,

but he was lush with other human traits, like the need to crush those soft lips under his.

Not that he would. The abyss churned painfully. His twin was dead wrong, he decided. This woman was not his responsibility. He'd never take another's love or happiness in his hands again or depend on someone else for his. He'd learned that lesson early on.

Shortly before his seventh birthday, his parents, plus his father's twin and another woman, had died in a freak storm while visiting the family homestead. Uncle Nick, the oldest of the three original Dalton brothers, and Aunt Milly had been saddled with six kids to raise in addition to their own daughter. Less than two years later, that daughter disappeared from the site of a tragic accident that had claimed her mother's life and hadn't been seen since.

A fierceness ripped through Travis. Uncle Nick had sacrificed to provide a home for the orphaned youngsters. He'd never expressed a single regret for taking them in. How had he stood it after losing his own wife and child?

The sound of a zipper being closed reminded him that morning would arrive all too soon. Then he'd have to do something about his stubborn guest. He checked the perimeter of the camp, then went to his tent.

Yeah, trouble, he thought when he was inside. Written in all caps.

* * *

Don't!

Alison woke to the sound of her own panicky voice. She felt as if she was being smothered. She pushed against the material that covered her face. Sobbing, she tried to fight clear, but she was hopelessly bound in something. Finally she managed to sit up. The sleeping bag fell to her waist.

A shadow, large and menacing, brushed by the tent. A bear! She yelled to make it go away.

"Hey, hey, take it easy," a masculine voice spoke from the darkness.

The zipper slid open and strong arms enclosed her in warmth and safety.

"I thought there was a bear," she murmured, trying to still her pounding heart. She was embarrassed as reality rushed in. "I was dreaming."

"You scared the pants off me when you yelled."

Alison rested against him, needing his strength for a moment. "The sleeping bag was over my face. It became part of my dream. There was danger all around, and I was alone."

"It's okay," he said. "You're safe."

Inhaling deeply, she caught the scent of him and lemon-fresh clothing, then more subtly, the faint aroma of aftershave lotion and talc, and fainter still, the masculine essence of him and his warmth.

Against her ear, she heard the steady pound of his heart as he held her close. She felt the strength of his enclosing embrace. Under her palm, she caressed the smoothness of bare flesh. She explored further and discovered wiry hairs in a rough diamond across his chest.

"Aren't you cold?" she asked in a near whisper.

"No."

Slowly, as if still in a dream, she tilted her head against his arm.

His face was a lighter shadow against the deeper one of the tent. The sudden tension between them made the air grow thicker and more difficult to breathe.

"Travis," she said, the name falling experimentally from her lips, as if it was an exotic word, foreign to her.

She heard him exhale, a slight hissing sound between his teeth, and felt the quick rise of his chest against hers as he inhaled. The movement of his head gave warning a second before his lips met hers.

Sound rose to her throat—a protest, a demand, she wasn't sure which—and she clung to him as if he was her anchor to sanity as a matrix of wildness stirred to life deep inside. It was like being caught in a whirlwind.

Sensation poured over her. The firmness of his lips against hers. The hard pound of his heart, echoing the beat of her own. The intimate mingling as his tongue sought hers and she opened to him, seeking the honey of his mouth as he did hers.

Softness washed over her, making her boneless and pliable. They slid downward until the sleeping bag puffed gently around her. His arm cradled her head, and his long frame partially covered her body.

The kiss deepened, becoming almost unbearable as pleasure rushed through her, wave upon wave of it, lifting her to heights she'd only read about. She felt his hand at her side, then the soft rasp of the zipper. He pulled the sleeping bag from between them. She found he was wearing thermal knit underwear that covered his lower body like skin, smooth and luxuriant to the touch.

His hand skimmed down her side and paused at her waist. With a gentle squeezing motion, he kneaded desire into her until flames seemed to spiral from his fingers right to her innermost being.

She kissed him just as fiercely, letting her hands roam his back and explore the solid muscles there. She trailed her fingers along his lean hips.

With a gasp, he moved against her, making her as aware of his passion as she was of her own. To her shock, she found she wanted to explore this tumult of sensation to the final reaches of desire.

When she writhed against him, he slid his hand upward until he cupped her breast. She felt the beading of her nipple as an intense pleasure. He murmured against her skin as he trailed kisses along her neck.

''What?'' she asked. ''What did you say?'' She found she wanted words, sweet words, magic words, promises...

Lifting his head, he stared down at her. ''What are

we doing? Just what the hell are we doing?'' he said in a voice filled with self-loathing.

The magic vanished. Sanity returned with a jolt Alison felt all the way to her soul. She scrambled away. He said a distinct curse, backed from the tent and zipped her inside once more.

''I'm sorry,'' she heard him say from outside, his tone rough with anger and regret.

''Don't be,'' she said, chilled to the bone. ''It was only...only a kiss.''

Chapter 4

Alison woke to luxurious warmth. The sun was shining on the tent, making it toasty warm. Dressing hastily, she crawled from the nylon dome and found Travis sitting beside the fire, a coffee cup cradled in his big hands. Gentle hands, she recalled.

A flush spread throughout her body. Last night, after regaining his sanity and apologizing for the kiss, he'd rekindled the fire, his movements restless and angry.

She wondered if he'd sat up all night, tortured by the brief passion they'd shared. Why did he resent it so?

''Good morning,'' she murmured when she took a seat close to the crackling fire. ''The sun feels good, doesn't it?''

He nodded. "Breakfast is in the skillet."

She helped herself to bacon and eggs and a sour-dough roll. Using her own fork, she ate, then cleaned the dishes.

"I'll take you back to town," he told her.

"I need my car."

He scowled impatiently. "I'll take you to your car, then escort you back to town."

"I'll go without an escort. How long do you think it will take you to find Janis?"

"That might be according to whether she wants to be found. A couple of days at most," he added when she started to protest the flippant reply.

"It's Friday, so I should hear from you on Sunday?"

He finished off his coffee, then stood. "You are the most persistent female I've ever met."

It wasn't a compliment.

She drained her cup, then rinsed and stored it in her backpack, now leaning against a tree. She packed the tent, which took as much effort as setting the thing up. Every item had to be folded and rolled to its minimum size in order to fit back in the nylon bag. It took two tries to achieve this feat.

Travis replaced the circle of soil and thin grass over the fire hole after drowning the embers. Alison realized that the casual observer wouldn't even notice the spot.

"Ready?" he asked.

With a sense of déjà vu, she nodded and fell into

step behind him on the faint trail that led downward. For a second, her gaze lingered on the little campsite as if to memorize the setting.

Nostalgia settled over her, and she experienced an intense longing for something undefined but very, very real.

Sighing, she admitted she didn't understand herself anymore.

Once more at the B&B, Alison promised Travis that she would stay put this time. "Until Sunday," she pledged. "If you…if Janis isn't here by then, I'm leaving."

"For home?" he asked hopefully.

"No, to find her."

"That's what I figured. Stay off the mountain, or I'll report you to the sheriff," he warned in a harsher tone than any he'd used previously with her.

"I don't respond to threats," she felt compelled to inform him, hearing the haughtiness in her tone.

"You're on my turf here. You'll do well to remember that."

Alison realized they were on the verge of a quarrel. From the front desk, she saw Amelia flick an inquiring, speculative glance their way, a smile at the corners of her mouth. The B&B owner probably thought they were having a lovers' spat.

Memories of last night's kisses flooded Alison without notice. Her eyes were irresistibly drawn to his lips, now compressed into a thin line of disapproval. Last night they had been mobile and sensuous, enticing her to follow his lead into passionate play.

Hunger swept through her, flooding her with needs stronger than she'd ever known. This fierce mountain man had opened up a void inside her, one she hadn't been fully aware of until two days ago. It was very disturbing.

"Well?" he demanded.

"I'm sorry. What did you say?"

He looked as if he could grind glass with his teeth. "I want your word that you'll do as I request."

For once.

The words were almost audible although he refrained from saying them. She couldn't help it; she smiled.

"What?" he demanded.

"It's just that we're so intense with each other. I mean…"

"I know what you mean."

His reply was spoken grudgingly. His eyes, locked on hers, admitted there was something different between them, something neither had encountered before. They blazed with blue fire, igniting the ready embers in her.

Her breath fluttered to her throat and seemed to die. She couldn't breathe, couldn't look away…

"What is this?" he demanded in a low tone only she could hear. "What the hell *is* this?"

She had no answer.

Without another word, he strode out, the door closing decisively behind him.

Amelia smiled and nodded to Alison as she passed the desk on the way to her room. The landlady wisely didn't comment on anything she'd seen or heard between the couple.

Suppressing a sneeze, Alison dropped her backpack inside the door and headed for the shower. She had a headache, and she needed to think. She did her best thinking under a stream of cleansing water.

On Monday, Travis photographed two beef carcasses for evidence, then left them to the buzzards. The birds pranced, wings spread, several feet away, impatient for him to be gone. Returning to the pickup, he tossed the camera into the glove box and headed for town.

He was tired, irritated and felt worse than death warmed over, as Uncle Nick would say. He sneezed four times in succession. A cold. Just what he needed.

After reporting the slaughter to the sheriff's office, he stopped by the B&B and discovered Alison had gone to lunch. Ignoring the amused gleam in Amelia's eyes, he asked her to have Alison call him at the ranch when she returned.

Outside, he decided to walk down to the local diner. Since there were only five places in town to eat, he could surely find her at one of them. Unless she'd gone shopping.

He suddenly recalled his mother had loved to shop, not to buy anything, but to look at the possibilities.

"When we get our mansion, we'll have one of those," she would say, pointing to a hot tub that cost five thousand dollars.

"Two," his dad would chime in. "One for the kids and one for us."

"I want one big enough to swim in," Travis had once told them.

"Well, of course, a heated pool, the very thing," his mom had agreed.

His parents had been dreamers, but they'd had so much fun as a family. A lump clogged his throat. What the devil had brought those old memories on?

"Hey, Travis," a rancher called out when he entered the small café that had served the town for over fifty years.

"Elmer," he acknowledged, stopping by the table where two longtime ranchers sat. "Hello, George," he said to the second man. The men were as gray-headed as Uncle Nick and as cantankerous.

"Any news on that riffraff hiding out in the woods?" Elmer wanted to know.

"Not a trace. They seem to be keeping to their end of the county."

"I found one of my bulls shot through the head two days ago," the rancher said. "Whoever did it took the haunches and left the rest. I filed a report over at the sheriff's office."

Travis spotted Alison at a table by a window. "Uh,

good. I have a report, too. Two of your neighbor's cows were slaughtered up near·She-Devil Mountain.''

The ranchers cursed. George told him, ''Those guys come on my land, they're going to regret it. I'm keeping a loaded shotgun close to hand.''

Travis was sympathetic. ''I know how you feel, but don't take the law into your own hands. You could get yourself killed. I've been tracking the men. They're staying on public land. See that your cattle don't stray.''

The ranchers grudgingly promised to check their fences. Travis told them to enjoy their meal and headed toward Alison's table. She watched him approach and take a seat, her mouth pursed into disapproving lines.

''You didn't find Janis,'' she concluded when he didn't speak at once.

''I had other fish to fry. There are paramilitarists in the area. They seem to have divided into two groups. From the paint-ball splatters, I'd say they are playing war games. The ranch has registered a business license for a game camp—''

''What does that mean?'' she interrupted.

''That Keith Towbridge, the grandson who inherited the land, intends to use the place as a vacation resort for war games and such. It's legal.''

''I see.'' She gazed out the window.

Travis noticed the way the sunlight, filtered through a light layer of clouds, hit her eyes, showing up the green outer circle and the smoky-gray flecks around the iris. He detected worry in their depths. What else was new?

"Personally, I don't see that your sister is in any kind of trouble. Other than some poaching of cattle—and we don't know who's doing that—I can't find anything illegal in this operation."

"That isn't the issue."

"I know. You need to find her because of your family concerns."

"If the ranchers and the pretend soldiers get in a shoot-out over some dead cows, people could get hurt. My sister, an innocent bystander, could end up dead."

"Not as long as they use paint balls for ammo."

"Those two ranchers you talked to won't be using fake bullets."

He had to give her credit for logic. "The military group is staying strictly in the mountains. They haven't been on any land but the Towbridge ranch or national forest. Your sister isn't involved in poaching."

She visibly relaxed. "That's good to know."

Travis yanked out a handkerchief and covered a sneeze. "Sorry. I've caught a cold."

She gave him a wry glance. "I have one, too. Those two nights in the woods must have done it."

Her words, spoken in a light, teasing voice, surprised him into recalling the moments of passion they had shared. He gazed into her eyes and saw an acknowledgment of the hot current that surged between them.

"I don't want this," he muttered in savage anger. "I can't go into my tent now without remembering—" He broke off, images of her snuggled up close to him, taunting him with her soft, feminine scent, coming to vivid life.

"I didn't know it would happen. I had the nightmare, then you were there, safe and comforting that second night. You came to my tent."

"We could have gone farther, much farther."

"We didn't."

The waitress brought him a menu and glass of water. He took a drink to relieve the tightness in his throat. That wasn't the only part of him that had reacted to the thought of them alone together up in the mountains.

"But we could have," he said when they were alone again. "I don't recall you telling me to stop. I'm not even sure why we had to."

"Because it wasn't wise," she told him, holding his gaze without backing down. "There was no point in it."

"Right," he agreed. "No point at all."

Except they had been a man and a woman intensely aware of each other, alone and filled with needs that refused to be suppressed. Why the waking of desire now? Why this woman?

"I heard you say cattle had been slaughtered. If not the paramilitarists, then who did it?"

He shrugged. "I found two sets of footprints at the site. Probably hikers who passed through the area and decided they needed fresh meat."

"That's a relief. Maybe Janis isn't involved in anything that could embarrass our father—"

Alison stopped, but the words had already fallen from her lips. She saw no surprise in Travis's eyes.

"That is," she began, trying to recover. She had never been so indiscreet in dealing with anyone before.

"I think I know how it is."

His voice was hard, but it seemed as soothing as hot cocoa on a cold morning, deep and rich and comforting.

Sometimes she felt as if she needed comforting. She couldn't figure out why.

Travis Dalton was a very attractive, masculine person. He was strong, at times gruff, but he had an innate sense of honesty and fairness. A man one could depend on.

She didn't know why that thought should console her. It wasn't as if *she* depended on him.

Travis rummaged through the kitchen cabinet where Uncle Nick kept the medicines. Finding the bottle of cold tablets, he shook two into his hand and swallowed them down. He felt miserable all over.

"Hey, bro," Trevor said upon entering the house. He spotted the pill bottle. "There's no medicine for a broken heart."

Travis groaned at the quip. He didn't feel up to dealing with his twin at present. He could see Zack outside, tossing a stick for one of the three dogs who lived on the ranch. The older brother lived in town, but came out to the ranch to work with the horses he raised when he wasn't chasing crooks for the sheriff.

"My heart is fine," he told his obnoxious sibling, deciding to leave as soon as his clothes came out of the dryer. He sneezed three times.

Trevor grinned. "I saw your girlfriend in town this morning. Funny, she was in the drugstore, stocking up on cold remedies. You sure nothing went on in that tent—"

Travis was in the twin's face in an instant. "Shut up about Alison."

Trevor held up his hands in mock surrender. "Please, don't shoot. I was only asking."

The quips made Travis see red. With supreme effort, he controlled the impulse to sock Trevor in the mouth.

"The only thing between her and me is concern for her sister's safety."

Trevor removed a bottle of medicine from the fridge. "Yeah?" He headed for the door. "Then we won't hear the patter of little feet around here next February? Too bad. I like kids."

The door banged shut.

Travis took a deep breath, then another, but it did no good. Following on his brother's heels, he caught up with him at the stable door. "You've stepped over the line,'' he warned, the fury a hot, welcome escape from his thoughts.

Trevor set the medicine bottle on top of a post. ''You have got it bad,'' he said. ''Hey, Zack, ol' Travis is in love.''

That's when Travis took a swing at him.

However, his brother ducked to the side and Travis swiped thin air. Zack came over to watch. Travis feinted with his right, then hooked with his left and got in a glancing blow.

Trevor put up his fists. ''You'll pay for that, little brother,'' he warned with a careless grin.

''You boys want a hiding?'' Uncle Nick demanded, coming out of the stable. ''Trevor, where's that medicine you were supposed to bring out?''

''On the post—''

Travis tackled his brother and they rolled across the ground. He felt like a good fight. He'd been wanting to pummel something for days. He realized he was taking his frustrations out on Trevor. Damn. He got to his feet and helped his twin up.

''Sorry, Trev,'' he began, then got socked in the eye. So much for apologizing. He tried for a headlock.

''Stop them,'' Uncle Nick ordered.

Travis felt hands grab him. His cousin Beau, coming out of the stable behind Uncle Nick, pinned his arm high on his back with a thumb hold. Zack did the same with Trevor.

''I don't know what's wrong with you two, fighting like a couple of kids.'' Uncle Nick glared at them.

Plainly disgusted, he said, "Last time you fought, it was over a girl Trevor took to the senior dance. What is it this time?"

Travis gave Trevor a threatening stare.

"A girl," Uncle Nick concluded as silence ensued. "Aren't you boys ever going to grow up?"

"I was trying to apologize," Travis muttered, "and got a poke in the eye for my efforts."

Trevor appeared contrite. "Sorry about that, bro. I didn't realize that things were serious between you and—"

"Nothing is serious," Travis immediately denied.

"Enough!" Uncle Nick roared. His eyes, true Dalton blue, raked over all four nephews. "If you need something to do, I can find a few chores to keep you busy."

Uncle Nick could assign enough work to wear the soles off a new pair of boots.

"Uh, I'm going to check on my mare," Zack said.

"Yeah, we need to give that horse her medicine," Trevor agreed. He and Zack ducked inside the stable.

"I've got to head back to the clinic for afternoon rounds," Beau, the doctor, stated, backing toward his pickup in the driveway.

"I'd better see about packing my clothes." Travis headed for the utility room next to the kitchen.

Within thirty minutes, he was on his way back to his hidden camp in the hills. He was going to get Janis Harvey to town if he had to kidnap the girl. Having seen the younger sister on TV a couple of times,

Travis knew she resembled Alison in coloring and facial features, so he wasn't worried about identifying her. He just hoped she wasn't as stubborn as her older sister.

He sneezed, blew his nose, then gingerly felt the soft tissue around his eye. He was glad he would be out of town and out of sight for the next few days so he wouldn't have to take any guff about a black eye. Upon consideration, he decided he would also be glad when the Harvey sisters were out of his hair.

The hollow blackness within stirred painfully. The world seemed to be shifting, so that up was down and down was up. He couldn't figure out what was happening to him.

Alison picked up a sandwich and carton of milk at the local deli and ate in her room. When Amelia invited her to join her for a glass of wine, she went willingly, needing to get away from her own thoughts.

Other guests were gathered in the large front room of the B&B where wine and snacks were served each evening. Amelia called out a greeting when she entered.

"Be with you in a minute," she said, placing a tray of hot hors d'oeuvres on a table. To Alison's surprise, the owner then led the way into a private area of the house. "Red, rose or white wine?"

"The cabernet will be fine." Alison looked around the sitting room. A place of wicker and chintz and colorful pillows, it was more casual than the lobby-reception area. Greenery lined the windowsills. African violets bloomed in many pots.

"You have a green thumb," Alison mentioned, indicating the flowers. "I can kill a silk plant."

Amelia laughed. "My grandmother showed me how to care for violets, so those are my one and only claim to gardening fame."

Alison sat in a comfy rocking chair and sipped the wine. Amelia served a tray of poppers and cheese sticks along with slices of Asian pear and kiwi fruit. The poppers, hot peppers filled with cheese, then battered and baked or fried, were the best Alison had ever eaten.

"Delicious," she told her hostess.

"From the frozen-food section at the grocery," Amelia said with a grin. "I do everything the easy way."

Alison nodded. "Good thinking."

"So how's your search coming along?"

"Search?"

Amelia shot her a rueful glance. "A lone female doesn't wander off into the hills unless she's very, uh, outdoorsy, which you're not, or on a mission. You being the senator's daughter would indicate the latter."

Alison sighed. She had always tried to maintain a low profile. "You knew who I was all the time?"

"Actually, I wasn't positive, but the last name was the same and I saw you on TV during the election. Plus, you have your father's eyes and light hair."

"You didn't say anything."

"Well, I figure, whatever you're doing here, it's your business." She grinned. "What *are* you doing in these parts?"

"Looking for my sister. She's on vacation at some ranch in the mountains, which I can't find."

"So Travis is helping," her hostess concluded. "Don't worry. If anyone can find your sister, Travis will. The Daltons know these hills better than anyone. They've hunted every inch of land in the Seven Devils range."

"Legally?" Alison asked, unable to hide her interest in the Dalton clan.

Amelia shrugged. "They've never gotten into trouble with the law that I know of."

"Do all six of the cousins live at the ranch?"

"No. Three are in Boise. Zack is a deputy sheriff for the county and has a room here at the B&B. The twins are the ranchers and they do some prospecting, I think. They're both volunteer deputies, too."

She tried to sound casual. "Are any of them married?"

Amelia shook her head. "Travis was, but his wife died in childbirth, along with the baby."

Alison was so shocked she couldn't speak for a moment. "How terrible for him," she said at last. The air about her became fragile, so that she had to breathe carefully to keep it from shattering.

"Julie was his childhood sweetheart. I think they fell in love in first grade. He changed after her death.

He's tasted sadness. His brothers and cousins haven't, not in that sense. Well, except when their parents died.''

Unable to stop, Alison probed and discovered that the cousins' parents had died while home on a visit. A heavy wet snow laid down over a light fluffy one had resulted in an avalanche, which swept their vehicle away like a cork caught in a tidal wave. A house-size boulder had crushed the pickup they were in.

''That's how all of them came to live with their uncle. He added more rooms to the original cabin on the ranch and kept all of them.''

''Uncle Nick must be a saint.''

Amelia laughed outright at this. ''If he is, he's an odd one. He's sort of crotchety and very plainspoken. He loved the ranch and settled on it while his brothers went off to make their fortunes following the rodeos. Unfortunately, there wasn't the money in them then as there is today.''

''So they never struck it rich?'' Alison asked.

''Right. The uncle shouldered all the financial problems of raising six additional kids as well as the emotional ones, in spite of his own tragedy shortly after that. Did you know his wife died in a car wreck and his daughter disappeared at the same time? She was only three or four.''

''What happened to the daughter?''

''No one knows. The sheriff thought she'd been kidnapped at the accident site. She was never seen again. They found footprints next to hers, but no one knew whose they were. It's been an unsolved mystery for over twenty years.''

Alison was silent for a minute as she absorbed this information. ''Travis and his twin turned out all right, so their uncle must have done a good job with the orphans in spite of his own losses.''

''They kept each other in line. If one misbehaved, the other five beat him up.''

''Five? Did the sister join in?''

''Whatever the Daltons did, they did together.''

Alison managed to laugh, not without a little envy of the close-knit family. ''The Daltons of Seven Devils Mountains. Sounds like an old Western movie.''

''Yes, but are they the good guys or the outlaws? The local folks have often wondered about this, especially at Halloween when the boys used to pull a wagon across the roof beam of a barn if the ranchers were so foolish as to leave their equipment outside.''

Again Alison felt the twinge of envy. Not that she hadn't had fun in her life, too, but a politician's child had to think of the consequences of foolish acts. She and Janis had been taught early to be aware of their duties in that regard.

For a moment, she envisioned how life might be if one were free to sample all the possibilities. To laugh with abandon. Maybe to go a little wild and not have to worry about what people would say. To fall in love without having to justify one's choice.

Not that she was in love, she quickly amended, but

to be free to love whom she wished seemed a wonderful luxury.

Her mother pushed the young lawyers and aides in her father's Washington, D.C., office in her direction, but she'd never fallen in love with any of them.

She'd had a high school steady but that hadn't worked out. Later, another man had said he loved her, but she'd soon realized he was more interested in her father's position and achieving his own ambitions than he was in love with her.

She'd even considered marrying him, but some remnant of a long-ago dream had held her back. She'd stopped believing in fairy tale romances before that, but there had been a faint hesitation, as if she knew she would forever lose something precious if she took that final step.

Observing the stars as they gathered in the night sky, she wondered if she hadn't already lost that part of herself.

Thinking of Travis's loss, she asked, "When did Travis lose his wife and baby?"

"It was two years ago. Two years this month."

Alison considered the darkness inside him and the anger he used to cover it. Travis had fallen in love, married and fathered a child. And had lost them.

The fragile air broke apart in her lungs, sending shards of pain through her chest.

"Excuse me," she said and went to her room as darkness fell across the wild beautiful land.

Chapter 5

Alison hit the off button on the alarm clock. Five o'clock wasn't her favorite time of day. Gritting her teeth, she rolled out of the warm bed and headed for the shower.

Today was Tuesday.

She'd warned Travis that she intended to go look for her sister if he hadn't found Janis by now. Actually she'd given him until Sunday and then had waited all day yesterday, an extra day, for word from him.

So why this niggling sense of guilt?

Stopping by the front desk, she left an envelope addressed to Travis, advising him of her intentions, which assuaged the guilt that ate at her. She couldn't wait around here forever.

Thirty minutes later, she slipped out to her car and crept out of town like an escaping criminal. When she'd arrived last Tuesday—had it really been a week ago?—she'd figured on finding Janis on Wednesday and heading home on Thursday. She *hadn't* counted on a run-in with Travis Dalton, rancher, prospector and volunteer deputy, or that her younger sibling would hide out in the wilderness.

Everything she'd learned since arriving in Lost Valley had reinforced her fears that Janis was mixed up in something not quite legit. What it was, she couldn't begin to imagine, but she had a bad feeling about it.

At the end of the road, she checked her gear and food supplies, then donned the backpack and headed up the tiny creek that flowed by Travis's camp. The trail she wanted to travel was closer that way than by following the road and taking the other trail farther north of here.

Finding Travis's camp was no problem for her this time. She was becoming an adept mountain woman.

Resting on the log Travis had provided, she ate a handful of trail mix, her thoughts going to the two nights she'd spent here with her reluctant rescuer.

A fist squeezed her heart as she gazed at the camouflaged tent under the pine boughs. Travis might act gruff, but there had been gentleness in him when he'd comforted her after the nightmare. For those few moments, it had been wonderful to lean against him and feel his strength and innate kindness.

The passion had been a surprise, for him as much as her. His lips had been warm and supple, moving against her mouth, hesitantly at first, then firmer as the hunger seized them both. It had been a long time since she'd been so attracted to a man. She'd wanted to forget everything and simply let the desire take them where it would.

Fortunately it hadn't, not quite. As her mother had reminded her last night, she was a practical, level-headed person. Family obligations were her first concern.

Funny, only Travis had ever made her forget duty completely. Those moments in his arms had been the sweetest interlude, the haunting notes of an all-too-brief melody heard from a distance.

An odd, nostalgic sadness engulfed her.

A minute later, a birdcall reminded her she must be on her way. She sighed as she rose and headed for the northern trail by the path she and Travis had followed. It wasn't a well-defined track, but she found, by careful observation, it was fairly easy to detect.

She had to smile at this new sense of accomplishment. Travis would surely have been impressed.

Right after he got over being furious.

The sun was inching toward a western peak when Alison finally reached the crest of the mountain, stopped and gasped. The view was spectacular.

The land dropped away in jagged ridges into a gorge. Hells Canyon—a place of ancient myths and timeless dreams, of glacier-scoured cirques and arêtes—an area as unforgiving as Everest in its indifference to humans.

Gazing at the ruggedly beautiful scene, she experienced an excruciating yearning to embrace the land and its vastness. Its lonely beauty weighed heavily in her breast, reminding her that once she'd been young and full of dreams.

Where had those dreams gone?

"I don't know," she said to the wind as it rose from the gorge and tousled her hair.

The words were whipped away into the mournful silence. She frowned, then smiled. She wasn't ancient, but she was old enough to know where dreams belonged.

Reality was a rocky trail and long hours of hiking. She'd better get with it rather than standing there on a lonely crest mooning over fantasies better forgotten. She pushed on.

Sometime later, she took a long break, shrugging out of the backpack and propping it against a sturdy tree. After drinking deeply from her canteen, she selected a seat on a log in a shady spot and rested her back against the tree.

Munching on trail mix, she mused on a trip through the mountains with a special person. Right, Annie Oakley meets Frank Butler in the Great Outdoors and lives happily ever after. Ha.

After checking the topography maps, she decided she was on the right track to intersect the ranch house that was supposed to be in the next valley to the north. If she ever got that far.

A sound came to her on the breeze, that of a voice speaking irritably. She listened intently. Someone was on the trail and coming her way.

She crouched under a low-hanging fir branch where she could see the trail clearly. Her heart quickened as the men came closer. There were two of them, both middle-aged, both panting from the climb. They didn't appear to be locals.

"There's nobody on the trail," one man griped.

"I saw something from below," his companion replied. "Let's go to the top of the ridge before turning back."

She heard them coming closer, then the footsteps stopped. A chill raced along her spine. She waited, not sure what to do. "Well, what have we here?" one man said.

Alison realized she'd been spotted. She rose. The two men gaped at her, their faces identical with comical surprise. "You're not the commandos," the bald one stated.

She assumed an air of confidence. "No, I'm not. I'm on my way to the Towbridge ranch."

"Who are you?" the taller of the two wanted to know. He shifted his position, blocking her on one side.

She stepped back. "Alison Harvey. I'm trying to get to the ranch. My sister is there."

"What's your sister's name?"

Alison hesitated, then told them. "Janis."

The man with the receding hairline nodded. "She's the cook."

Cook? Janis? Alison didn't have the foggiest idea what this meant, but she decided it was better to act as if she understood. "Then this is the correct trail to the ranch?"

"Yep, just follow it down to the camp. Keep going north when the trail forks."

"It's time we were getting back," the other man remarked. "You can come with us," he told Alison.

She wondered if she should. The men seemed harmless, but looks could be deceiving. Remembering her mission, Alison gripped the bear-spray can and nodded. "Would you mind introducing yourselves?" she asked pleasantly.

"I'm Merv," the taller man said. "This is Harry."

"Glad to meet you. Are you with a paramilitary group?"

Merv snorted. "We're playing at being soldiers, but we're just a bunch of overweight businessmen up here on a retreat. The company thinks this will teach us to be resourceful, think out of the box and improve our teamwork."

Harry, the balding one, nodded. "So far, all I've gotten is blisters from these hiking boots."

Alison relaxed as they laughed ruefully. She fell into step between the men when Merv indicated she and Harry should go first. As they marched along, she planned the coming meeting with her sister and how she should present the facts concerning their father. The simple truth was the best way, she decided.

"Almost there," Harry said after a half-hour walk.

Anxiety rippled through her as they left the trees and entered a small plateau tucked up against a high ridge of layered rock. A picnic table with a camp stove on it stood next to a cooking pot hung over a fire pit. Short sections of logs supplied the seats. A cabin stood to one side of the clearing.

A woman, dressed in denim coveralls and a man's plaid shirt, sat at the table. Her hair was pulled back with a blue scrunchy. She looked like a country girl, fresh-faced and wholesome. She was smiling as she turned toward them. The smile froze on her face.

"Janis!" Alison said and rushed forward, relief at finding her sibling bringing her close to tears.

"How did you get here?" Janis demanded, disbelief and anger flashing into her eyes.

"What do you mean, gone?" Travis demanded. He looked from Alison's ridiculous note to the B&B owner.

Amelia shrugged. "As in, she left early this morning. With her backpack. I saw her from my bedroom window when she got in her car around five-thirty."

"Both of you were up that early?" he asked, hoping this was a joke. He felt dangerous, on the brink of an explosion he was so furious with Alison and her stubborn dedication to her task.

"I always get up at five-thirty," Amelia said defensively. "I have work to do."

"Sorry, I didn't mean to sound like a bear, it's just…" He couldn't say exactly what was eating at him. "It's stupid for someone to go off into the hills alone and without a clue about the danger. Hypothermia kills more hikers a year than grizzlies have in the last hundred."

At Amelia's assessing stare, he shut up. A flush warmed his neck and ears. His glare dared her to make a smart remark. "I suppose I'll have to go find her," he said.

"Yes, I suppose you will," she said, a gleam dancing in her eyes.

Cursing silently, he thanked Amelia and left the B&B. He'd planned on returning to the gold mine. The vein was small and wouldn't take long to pan out. Now he'd have to track into the mountains before Alison got herself into real trouble.

His heart pounded all of a sudden, startling him.

Thinking of the politician's daughter and the passion she'd induced got his insides all twisted. She was everything he knew to stay away from in a woman, but the hunger lingered, taunting him at odd moments.

For a second he considered an affair with her. It would be brief and hot, then she'd go back to the city and he'd head for the hills again. However, passion could lead to complications, and he didn't need those.

He found her car exactly where he'd expected. After hiding his truck, he donned his gear and started out. When he caught up with her, she was going to be in big trouble.

Hopping across the creek from boulder to boulder, he searched for her tracks on the other side. No new ones. He used his flashlight to highlight the trail. Nothing.

Cursing, he returned to her car. There he picked up her fresh footprints and carefully followed every move she made. To his surprise, she'd gone up the creek.

An hour later, Travis approached his campsite silently. He wanted to catch her off guard and thus teach her a lesson on forest safety. She deserved to have the pants scared off her. When the camp was in full sight, he stopped and observed the area. Where the hell was she?

Giving her five minutes in case she'd heeded nature's call, he leaned a shoulder against a tree and waited. Within a minute, he knew she wasn't in the vicinity. He could feel the emptiness of the place.

Checking the campsite, he saw she'd eaten something, probably trail mix. He studied the raisin on the ground beside the log as if it could give him a clue to her perverse female mind.

Yanking a candy bar out of his pocket, he ate it as he picked up her path, this time heading up the obscure game trail that would take her farther into the wilderness. He followed her footprints without a problem.

Finally he breached the crest of the trail and started

down. He paused and surveyed the crenellated valley far below. Other valleys veered off the main one as far as the eye could see. This was the Nez Perce National Wilderness, which was part of the Payette National Forest.

Thousands of acres of mountains, valleys and trees spread out before him, covering the copper-rich deposits the area was known for. Glacier-gouged lakes abounded—Black, Emerald and Baldy being the best known.

He'd search every damn inch if he had to.

Going a few steps, he stopped abruptly, then bent forward and studied the rocky, slightly wider place in the trail. Two sets of footprints had joined Alison's, one on each side of her.

She'd been waylaid by two guys wearing heavy-tread boots. The prints told him the whole story. She'd tried to back up, but the men had her trapped. The three had headed downhill, single file with her in the middle.

Something akin to panic bit deep into his gut. An urge to run down the dangerous slope as fast as possible fought against the self-control he'd learned at a young age.

Hell, there wasn't a body lying in the trail, so why was he getting himself tied into a knot? There wasn't even signs of a struggle.

Travis studied the men's prints so he could easily recognize them. Hiking and combat boots, most likely purchased at an army-navy store, he concluded. Pretend soldiers. Just what the world needed more of.

He checked his weapons, made sure they were fully loaded although he didn't chamber a shell, and hooked a spare can of pepper spray on his belt. He had a full stash of ammo in his backpack. Moving fast but carefully, he pushed deeper into the wilderness.

A coldness entered his blood, chilling his thinking processes until every one of his five senses were as sharp and clear as ice crystals. He forged ahead, his eyes constantly on the alert for danger.

When it was too dark to risk a mishap on the steep, downward grade, he tossed a tarp over some pine boughs, slid into his sleeping bag after eating a helping of trail mix and bedded down.

Before going to sleep, he thought of other nights spent in the mountains. The emptiness of his life over the past two years seemed to expand until it filled the vast darkness of the night sky. He was no stranger to loneliness, but tonight it seemed more profound....

''Why did you come?'' Janis continued.

Merv and Harry glanced at the two women, then muttered about having something to do and moved to the far side of the clearing, giving the sisters some privacy.

Alison dropped her backpack and rushed around the table. Janis held both hands up, palms out, when Alison would have dropped to her knees to hug her.

The action, coming on top of the difficult hike and the week of worry, cut deeply. Alison retreated to the other side of the hewn-log table. She felt discouraged and unsure about why this trip had seemed so important, why she'd been so driven to find this cool stranger whose welcome was anything but friendly.

"Everyone was worried about you," she said, finding it difficult to speak. "Your cell phone stopped working."

"I had it turned off. It was too expensive."

"I'm sure Father would take care—"

"There was no one I wanted to talk to," Janis interrupted. Her eyes, usually a warm, lively gray with a green outer edge, were mutinous.

Alison fought to not be offended. She was used to her sister's defiant ways.

"You're needed at home," she said in a calm, soft voice that wouldn't carry to the men. "Father is ill."

The anger disappeared. "Ill? With what?"

Alison explained quickly. "He has a tumor at the base of his skull. He refuses to have it removed until you're home. You must come," she finished.

Janis hesitated, then said, "This is a trick to get me to go back, isn't it? I don't believe Father has any such thing. Who told you about it?"

"Mother. No one else knows."

"Ah, yes," Janis said as if it all became clear.

She seemed older and sadder, too, in a way Alison had never noticed. With something like shock, she saw her sister as a person separate from the family, one determined to have a life apart from them.

"Father isn't a fool," Janis continued in a low voice. "He has access to the best medical advice in the world. If he were really ill, he'd have already had it taken care of. You've wasted your time coming here. Tell Mother that when you see her."

Alison hadn't expected this to be easy. Dealing with her family never was. She would simply have to convince Janis to do the right thing.

"I want you to leave," Janis said.

Alison blinked. When she spoke, it was in her most reasoned manner. "I can't return today. It's too late."

Janis's lips thinned in anger, but before she could speak, a male voice chimed in. "She's right."

A man Alison had never seen entered the clearing from a path through the trees. He was young, no more than twenty-five or so. He wore jeans and a T-shirt with boots and a cowboy hat. His hair was medium brown with sun streaks. His eyes were brown and had an earnest expression as he glanced from her to Janis.

He stopped beside Janis and laid a hand on her shoulder. "She'll have to spend the night," he said.

Janis swung her legs around the seat and pushed herself to her feet. "I don't want her here."

Alison didn't react to the last statement. Instead, she gasped aloud, her eyes glued to her sister's abdomen.

"Yes, I'm pregnant," Janis said, her chin tilted at a proud angle. She slipped an arm around the man and leaned against him. He held her close in a protective embrace.

For once, words failed her. Finally she asked, "Are you...you two are married?"

The man answered. "We're committed to each other. I'm Keith Towbridge. You must be Alison."

She nodded.

He smiled rather solemnly. "I'm glad to meet you."

Her sister spoke. "Well, now that the truth is out, I suppose you can't wait to call Mom and Dad and spread the word."

"Don't you want them to know?" Alison couldn't fathom leaving one's family out of such important news. Slowly she gathered her composure. "You surely didn't think you could hide your condition forever."

Janis shrugged indifferently.

"When are you due?" Alison asked.

"July. The twenty-ninth," Keith answered after a short silence.

Two and a half months to go. *A baby. Dear God.* "Have you seen a doctor?" she asked Janis.

"It's none of your business." At a glance from Keith, she added impatiently, "Yes, and I'm fine."

Alison stood rooted to the spot while Janis went to the fire pit. She removed the lid from a kettle and stirred a big pot of stew. The hearty aroma reminded Alison that she'd only had trail mix in the last several hours. She started to offer her help, but thought better of it.

Slowly she sank to the rough log stool. There was so much to think about—the baby, her parents' shock when they found out, her own sense of responsibility, as if she'd somehow failed her little sister by not seeing this disaster coming and averting it.

A baby. She would be an aunt. Janny, little Janny, a mother. Her baby sister.

Somehow she had to think this through, figure it out and… What to do? They had to do something…

The irony of the situation hit home. This was life as usual in the Harvey family. Janis resented any interference while Alison tried to keep the peace between the family members.

A baby. This was more than youthful rebellion.

She stared at the couple. Keith had moved over beside Janis, his stance cautious, his eyes wary, his every gesture protective of the woman who stirred the cook pot.

Turning toward the deepening twilight and last glory of the sunset fading beyond the far horizon, Alison suddenly wished she could walk away and never, never look back.

"Dinner is ready. Did you meet our guests?" Keith asked her politely.

"Two of them. They found me on the trail and showed me the way here. They said they were on a company retreat."

Keith nodded. "We teach strategy and teamwork,

then have war games with two armies to develop skills. I'm in charge of operations on this end.''

''I see.''

''You don't approve,'' Janis stated, reading more in her stiff posture than was there. ''Women don't, but it's a guy thing.'' She shrugged.

''Do you have a place to sleep?'' Alison asked, looking around the sparse encampment, seeking practical matters to occupy her mind until she could think more clearly.

A baby. She couldn't think of a thing to do about that.

Janis eyed her backpack. ''Didn't you bring a tent?''

''We'll put her in the cabin,'' Keith told Janis in a firm tone. ''We have a house,'' he said to Alison. ''You can stay with us. This way.''

Grabbing her pack, he led the way to an old ranch house. Behind it, the overhang of a gigantic cliff offered protection from the north wind. She heard water rushing over stones and realized a creek must be close.

''An underground spring runs at the back of a cave in the rocks. We're in the watershed of the Snake River. You can hear the roar of the rapids if you listen. The Salmon runs into the Snake north of here.''

A shiver rushed over her. The Salmon River was also known as the River of No Return because it was so rough and dangerous. Once down it, there was no way to go back upriver. The mountain men had returned on a southerly route.

"Why did you bring Janis here?" Alison asked, her gesture indicating the camp and all it represented.

"We want to revive the ranch. No one has lived here for over twenty years, but I remember visiting when my granddad was alive. It's a good place to raise a family. The retreat was a friend's idea to provide cash flow while we get started. We're working on the house."

Alison recognized the glow of a long-held dream as he recounted the plan. Her sister had evidently bought into it, too. Saying nothing, she followed him inside.

The house was four small rooms, all connected by doors leading from one to the other. The first one was the living room. The kitchen was right behind that. The other two were bedrooms, used mostly for storage.

"I'll clear a place in here for you." He went into the bedroom immediately to the right of the living room.

Following, she saw stacked bunk beds against one wall. He put her backpack down and removed some boxes and blankets from the lower bunk, placing the items in chairs that were already piled high with household things.

"There's electricity," he said and flipped the switch.

A light fixture mounted on the ceiling came on.

"Thank you." Alison managed a smile. "This will do nicely. I thought I would have to sleep in a tent tonight."

"I'd better help with dinner. There's a bathroom beyond the other bedroom. Uh, the well isn't hooked up yet, but there's water in a bucket. Join us when you're ready."

Alison explored the house after he left. The kitchen was being remodeled. A new stove and dishwasher waited to be installed. The wall had been repaired where the old stove had stood. New cabinets were already in place.

While this work showed promise, it was still a small, rather primitive abode. She couldn't imagine her sister living here for very long. With a baby to care for, it would be even harder. She hurriedly washed up, using water from the bucket, then returned to the picnic table.

Janis was alone. She gave Alison a wary glance, then set plates and forks on the table. After a few minutes of silence, she spoke. "Go ahead and yell at me before you explode," she advised sarcastically.

Alison inhaled slowly. "Why?" she asked. "Why go off without a word to anyone? Surely you knew we would worry."

"I wanted to be with Keith."

"You only have another year of college. Couldn't you have waited until you graduated to start the pioneer life?"

Janis grimaced. "I'd flunked economics—"

"Oh, Janny."

Her glance was scalding. "I never wanted to take it in the first place. That was Dad's idea."

Alison nodded. There'd been many quarrels over school and grades and spending money. Father would yell, Mother would retreat to her room with a headache, Janis would threaten to leave home forever. Alison would sweep up the pieces of family life and put them together again.

"Anyway, I met Keith. He was working in construction and saving his money to start the ranch. We realized we didn't want to be apart, so I came with him."

Alison stared at her sister's enlarged body. "Without a word to the parents," she reminded the younger woman.

"I called you a couple of times." She flicked Alison an angry glance before stirring the stew again. "You could have told me you were coming."

"How? You said there was no phone at the ranch. You turned your cell-phone service off."

"We're on a tight budget."

"Can you afford the baby?"

Janis laughed. "Well, he's on the way, no matter what."

"He?"

"It's a boy."

"Do you need money for the doctor?"

The aloof coldness returned. "Keith will help me with the delivery."

This took a moment to sink in. "You're going to have the baby at home?"

"Don't look so shocked. Babies were born for thousands of years without hospitals and doctors and modern medicine."

"A lot of them didn't make it through the first year, either," Alison retorted and was immediately ashamed. "I'm sorry. I didn't mean—"

"I'm not worried. I'll have Keith. He loves me, and he's all I need." Janis shot Alison a proud glance. "We have checked with a doctor in town. Everything looks fine. His nurse is a midwife. She'll come when it's time."

Alison refrained from asking how they planned on contacting the midwife. She felt disoriented, as if she'd stepped into another time, another place. She no longer recognized her sister in this very pregnant young woman who cooked over an open fire.

Where was the Janis who'd never learned to boil water, as far as Alison could recall?

"This is all very romantic and pioneering," Alison said, smiling in sudden understanding.

Janis whirled around. "Don't," she said. "Don't make fun of it. This is Keith's and my dream, to make a go of this place that no one in his family wanted to keep but him. We can build a life here. And we will!"

"I wasn't going to ridicule your ideas. I'm just worried about you and the baby," Alison murmured.

"Don't be. I want to do this. For once, I want to

do something without worrying about Father's career. I'm so *tired* of his damn career."

Keith appeared with a bucket of water and placed it on the table. He put an arm around Janis when she leaned against him and rested her head against his shoulder.

Alison thought of arms that had enclosed her when she'd had the nightmare. She wished someone was there to offer her comfort now as Keith did for Janis.

An image came to her—dark hair and eyes as blue as the sky, someone like her, who'd lost his dreams...his wife...his child...

A baby. Oh, dear Lord.

Chapter 6

Breakfast came early the next morning. Keith did the cooking on a camp stove set up on the end of the picnic table. Alison joined him and the other two men in the chilly dawn light. Her sister didn't appear.

They had all gone to bed shortly after dark the previous night. Through the thin walls of the cabin, Alison had listened to the whispered conversation between Keith and Janis, unable to understand the words but recognizing her sister's stubborn anger as the couple argued.

Over her being there, she'd presumed.

She inhaled deeply and tried to ignore the ache, both physical and mental, that had stayed with her during the night. She'd never felt so unwanted and unnecessary and unsure about what she should do.

Before she began the long hike out, she decided she would talk to Keith about a phone, and the future. There were a couple of questions she wanted to put to him.

Finished with the meal, she helped clean up while the company men drank their coffee. Both were quiet. Harry carved on a cedar stick while Merv puffed on a cigarette.

This was the peaceful scene that greeted Travis when he strode into camp. He cast an assessing glance over the four people at the table. "This certainly looks cozy," he said.

He couldn't decide if Alison was surprised to see him or not. He gave her a mock-menacing scowl. "I thought I told you to stay put, that I'd find your sister." Including the men in an exasperated grin, he added, "Women, they never do what they're told."

The youngest of the three men rose and held out a hand. "I'm Keith Towbridge. You know Alison and Janis?"

"Travis Dalton," he said, shaking hands. "I know Alison. The Seven Devils Ranch, over the ridge in the next valley, is our spread. I didn't know anyone was living over here until Alison came looking for her sister."

"Janis and I are rebuilding—"

Before he could say more, all hell broke loose. Several men, whooping like banshees, dashed into the clearing from the trees, surrounding the area. They wore cammies and had black streaks on their faces. All of them toted rifles.

During the first moments of confusion, Travis shoved Alison under the table. He shielded her with his body while he pulled a .38 semiautomatic from a belt holster.

She laid her hand over his. "War games, I think."

"Don't move or you're dead," one of the men shouted.

Travis lifted his head above the edge of the table in order to take a quick count of the enemy. A shot rang out and almost immediately a stinging sensation hit his side. He glanced down at the spot and saw a blob of yellow start to drip down on his pants leg.

"Drop your weapon," the leader of the group told him. He chuckled gleefully. "We got the whole bunch."

Travis holstered the gun, helped Alison to her feet and turned on the leader of the pretend soldiers. "Don't you know better than to raid a camp when women and strangers are present? I could have shot all of you. And my bullets are real." He swiped the paint off with a paper towel.

"Uh, at ease, men," the leader said. "We're Commando Unit Alpha. I thought we were supposed to capture you guys."

Keith spoke up. "You got us fair and square. I didn't think you'd be able to find our camp so soon."

Travis nodded to the commandos as Keith introduced them. "Travis here is a neighboring rancher.

We didn't get a chance to tell him about a possible raid.''

The new men settled on stumps and logs with fresh mugs of coffee and related their adventures of the past three days. It had taken them that long to track their comrades through two miles of wilderness and find their camp.

Travis was aware of Alison sitting beside him, a pleasant, attentive expression on her face as she listened to the tale of adventure in the wilderness. He knew on some basic level that it was a facade.

There was weariness in her pale face, as if she'd taken a serious blow and it was only a matter of time before it became a mortal one.

Someone had hurt her. He knew it on an instinctive level that had no bearing to reason and logic.

Big deal, he scoffed as some softheaded part of him wanted to take her in his arms and offer comfort. Live long enough and pain was inevitable. The fates loved to whack people down when they least expected it. Apparently Alison was just learning this lesson. If so, she'd had an easy life as far as he was concerned.

Where was the other Harvey girl? He had an impression of a spoiled brat in the younger sister, but what did he know? It wasn't as if his opinion meant a thing in the grand scheme of things. If he were wise, he'd keep his thoughts to himself and far from the woman who silently observed, her eyes deep pools of fortitude laced with profound worry.

She stirred beside him. ''More coffee?'' she asked.

He nodded and moved slightly to let her fill his cup, then her own. The heat from her body caressed his side as she stood close, her attention focused on the task.

A sudden, fierce need came over him. He didn't understand where it came from, only that it reminded him of the pain from the past and he didn't like it. Walking a few steps away, he swallowed a gulp of the strong, boiled cowboy coffee and surveyed the camp.

Earlier, he'd realized Alison wasn't in danger as he'd observed their morning meal—that's why he'd walked calmly into the clearing with the three men present—but he'd known there was a problem from the tension in her.

Eyeing the encampment, he wondered if the kid sister was in the old ranch house nestled in the trees. The two weekend warriors had been in the other cabin when he'd first arrived and scouted the place. Alison and Towbridge had been preparing breakfast.

When he'd walked into their midst, he'd seen a flash of welcome in her eyes, as if she'd been glad to see a friend. As if she'd needed one.

Not him, a part of him advised. He wasn't anyone's friend. He considered gathering his gear and heading for his own camp, far from the troubles of others.

"Have you had breakfast?" Alison asked.

"Not yet."

Indicating that he should sit in her place, she prepared scrambled eggs with quiet efficiency on the camp stove. Travis figured that was the way she did everything—with simple competence and no expectations of praise. She did her job, no fuss, no muss.

She toasted bread over the burner, then set the meal before him and asked if anyone wanted more coffee.

"Sure," Merv said. He pulled out a cigarette pack, peered inside, then sighed and put it away. "I'm supposed to quit these. My wife keeps a spray bottle handy. If she catches me smoking, she squirts water on me."

"A woman after my own heart," Alison said with a true smile that brightened the worry in her eyes.

"You gals are hard-hearted," Merv lamented.

Janis appeared while they were laughing. "What's so funny?" she asked.

Her grouchy tone put a pall over the table. Travis understood at once what Alison's problem was. The younger sister was in a delicate condition…and an embarrassing one for the senator. There was no ring on her finger to go with the bulge of her tummy.

Trouble with a capital *T.* Yeah. Thank heaven it wasn't his problem this time. He wondered how Alison was going to handle this "situation," as she diplomatically termed her family's crises.

"Feeling bad this morning?" Keith asked, giving Janis his stool.

"Just tired." Janis smiled at him before turning a hard gaze on Alison.

Alison was aware of Travis's comprehensive glance at the couple, then at her. Lifting her chin, she dared him to say anything. He merely raised his eyebrows as if asking what she was going to do now.

Well, she still hadn't come up with plan B, although she'd fretted about it the whole night. She intended to call and let the parents know she'd found Janis. She'd decided to let Janis explain her condition.

"I suppose we should start home soon," she said to Travis. "I'd like to get back to town before dark."

No one, including her sister, responded.

Alison felt a wrenching sense of personal failure. She felt burdened by it all—the difficult search for her sister, the expectations of her family that she would find Janis and somehow talk her into coming home, the ambitions of her father that drove them all.

Well, she had failed on the second part. During the night, she'd realized there was no way she could make the younger girl do anything. Perhaps she should wait until she was at the B&B to call her parents. That would give her time to think of what to say.

Travis shook his head. "We may as well rest for a day before starting back over that ridge. It's going to be a hard day's hike."

"I'm fine, if you're concerned about my making it."

His gaze ran over her, assessing her condition. While he concealed it better than her sister, Alison knew he didn't want her around, either. She stared into the steaming mug until pride could drive the sting of tears away.

"I want to scout out the area first," he continued.

"Because?"

"There might be an easier trail than over the ridge. I can see a saddle farther down the mountain. See that dip in the tree line over there?"

She followed his line of sight. "Yes."

"There used to be a logging road around the flank of the mountain and over that saddle. I have topography maps of the area. I'll study those and the lay of the land, then we'll decide."

Feeling her sister's hostile gaze, Alison cleared her throat and said, "I would rather go today."

Keith spoke to the other men. "If you men are ready, it's time you were starting back to the main camp."

"How did you get them in?" Travis asked.

Keith explained he had a partner and they had cleared and repaired an old road from the highway to a lodge they were building on the front side of the property.

"Shouldn't you take Janis over there? She's getting close to time, isn't she?" Travis asked.

"The lodge is only a foundation so far. There's no place for her to sleep. I'm fixing up the old ranch house. It'll be done before winter."

Travis frowned. "In that case, I'll get some help and clear the ford at the creek so you can get out that way."

Janis scowled at their helpful neighbor. "We don't need a road. I'm going to have the baby here."

Alison could have strangled her sister. She saw Travis's knuckles turn white as he gripped the mug. Memory washed through his eyes like a spring downpour, and she saw everything he'd once been in a glance—the loving husband, the delighted father-to-be, the man who had cared so much for his little family.

Overlaying all that was the man he'd become—the one filled with black desolation, his soul a wasteland that rejected anyone who came close. Now he had her problems to deal with.

Oh, Travis, I'm so sorry.

He shrugged. "It's your life."

"I wish others would remember that." Janis looked directly at Alison.

Alison kept her face expressionless as she returned the glare. In the silence that followed, the other guests recalled they were leaving. Merv and Harry said their farewells, gathered their backpacks from the cabin and took off a few minutes later with their commando buddies. Keith advised them on the correct trail to follow.

Janis went to the house while Alison volunteered to wash up the few dishes that remained. Travis brought out the topo maps. He and Keith studied them, then decided Travis should scout out the old road and see if it was passable.

Left alone, Alison finished her task, then explored the cliff area behind the house. She found the spring bubbling out of the rock at the back of a shallow cave.

Following its course as it became a creek meandering toward the river in the distance, she spotted a flint arrowhead among some rocky debris. She held it up to the sun and admired its translucent edges, carved by some skillful warrior long ago.

A yearning for another time welled up inside her. She longed for something she'd never known—a purpose, a sense of destiny, something, anything. Her breath tangled in a knot and she ceased to breathe as she waited, poised on the brink of a great discovery...

Finally she had to exhale, then she laughed softly, regretfully, at how absurd she was to stand there in the middle of a wilderness and expect a grand revelation. She walked on.

Travis scouted the area south of the camp most of the day. He found the remnants of the logging cut he sought. It was riddled with rocks, trees had sprouted down the middle, but with a little bulldozing, it could be made passable. It was also an easier walk to the ranch.

Hiking back to the old ranch quarters, his thoughts reverted to Alison's sister. Pregnant. Determined to deliver her baby at home. Stupid, stupid, stupid.

He clenched his fists as the worrisome thoughts chased themselves around and around his mind like a dog chasing its tail. It wasn't his problem, he added into the mix.

Dammit, it wasn't.

It was almost dark when he returned to camp. Alison rose and dished up a plate of fish and chips. "Keith gave me some tackle and showed me his favorite fishing hole. I caught three trout."

"You can fish?"

She nodded, a shyness in her smile as she explained that a gardener who had been with the family forever had taught her and Janis when they were little.

His stomach rumbled. "Looks great."

The food tasted as good as it looked. Watching Alison, seated across the table from him, he experienced a shift in the dark center at his core. Her quiet distress was not his doing. It was none of his business. This time, a woman's pain wasn't his fault.

"Where are your sister and Keith?" he asked over a cup of boiled coffee.

"Her back has been hurting today, so she stayed in the house. Keith has the water hooked up and was working on the new kitchen he's putting in."

Travis nodded. "I thought I'd see about helping him with the back road into this place from ours. Trevor and I can clear it with the tractor and lay down a bed of gravel from a bar along the creek."

A glow ignited in Alison. "Would you?" she asked. "I've been so worried. That would be such a help. With a good road, they can get to town in a hurry in case…in case they need to."

She realized where her tongue was taking her in time to change the words, but she saw the darkness in his eyes before they became expressionless once more. She'd been about to say, "in case something happens with the baby.'' He'd known what she was thinking.

Impulsively she leaned across the table and laid her hand over his. ''Thank you, Travis. Thank you for all your help.''

He nodded, then moved his hand away to lift the mug to his lips, his eyes as blue and cold as mountain glaciers.

The last of the light faded while they sat at the table. Suddenly a shadow swooped around her head, startling her. She batted at it.

''Don't,'' he said. ''Sit still. They won't hurt you.''

Bats dipped and darted all around them, grabbing insects in midair, their needle-sharp teeth ominous, but never once brushing against the two humans who watched, spellbound, as they worked.

It wasn't until the little creatures flew off that she spoke again. ''I'm going to bed.'' She hesitated, then nodded toward the newly constructed cabin. ''I moved my things there this afternoon so that Janis and Keith can have privacy. The cabin has bunk beds, four of them. It's okay, I mean, I don't mind if you share it.''

''Thanks.''

She couldn't tell anything from his tone. She hurried off without looking back. The idea of being alone with him didn't worry her nearly as much as the animosity she felt in the other house.

Better the devil you know...

She managed a mocking smile. Travis Dalton didn't want her any more than her sister did.

Chapter 7

It was well after dark before Travis decided he should go to bed. At the cabin, he knocked, announced himself and entered when she called it was okay for him to come inside. The interior was dark as a tomb.

Using his flashlight, he checked the place out. In the soft light, he saw Alison's clothing neatly folded and laid atop her hiking boots beside a bunk bed. From the bunk, she watched him with eyes that were shadowed with concern.

Not his problem, he reminded his conscience.

Sitting on the opposite bunk, he removed his boots and rubbed his tired feet. After turning off the flashlight and placing it under his pillow, he slipped off his outer clothing, leaving in place the thermal underwear he wore in the mountains. He heard a sigh.

Across from him, she was a slender outline within the sleeping bag. In the spill of moonlight through the windows, he saw her eyes on him, felt their pull, the magnetism that arced between them, knew her thoughts.

Heat rampaged through him. Hunger jumped on his flagging conscience and beat it into submission. He fought it, then crossed the few feet of space between them.

She was ready when he got to her. Her arms slipped from the cover and closed around him. Her mouth met his. No coy denial. No subterfuge. Just sweet, sweet hunger. Mutual hunger.

He tried to touch her all over, all at once, moving his hands here and there, exploring the womanly curves, reveling in the warmth that grew between them, becoming fiery as the need increased.

Pushing the zipper down, he slipped into her sleeping bag, tucking his thigh between hers, experiencing the full impact of her as he pressed closer, then eased.

"I could take you right here," he murmured, "and to hell with the consequences, I want you that much."

"I know." She kissed him all over his face, skimming his eyes, his nose, his lips, making him fiercely hungry for all of her. "But you don't want to."

Her honesty stilled his hands for a moment. "No," he whispered. "I don't want to. I don't want passion and need and wanting." He exhaled in defeat. "But I want *you*."

Under his hands, her thermals were silky smooth

and fit her curves like skin. He stroked her back, her sides, her belly. He captured her small but perfect breasts and exhaled sharply as her nipples beaded under his caress and she pushed upward to meet his touch.

Sliding over her, feeling her legs open then close over his hips, he pressed into that enticing notch and heard her moan sweet and low with pleasure. He took the kiss deeper.

Wildly, they moved as one, sensation strong in spite of the clothing that kept them from complete contact.

At last he eased the kiss, that cautious, unwilling part of him knowing it was time to stop while they still had some control. Sex with this woman wouldn't be merely sex. He couldn't, wouldn't, make it more.

So, it had to stop. But gently. He'd started this. He had to end it without hurting her.

He kissed her in several gentle forays and let them come down from the peak. For a minute there was no sound but that of their labored breathing. Then he shifted to the side and rose. Guilt ate at him as he slid the cover over her heated body.

"I'm sorry. That was a..." He tried to think of a word.

"Mistake," she supplied.

That honesty again. She was a woman who could face facts. "A mistake," he agreed, aware of the sexual gruffness in his tone that spoke of needs not quite met. He resented those needs. "Sleep. Tomorrow will be a long day."

To his surprise, she smiled. "I know."

He was once again aware of the courage in her, the sense of duty that drove her and the weary concern within her that was as haunting as the whispers of a lonely ghost.

Something shifted in him, a balance beam of emotion that had held steady for him these past two years. Grimly he settled in his bunk. He hadn't asked for this.

Alison woke before first light. Listening but not moving, she heard the woodstove door being opened and logs added. She peeked over the edge of her sleeping bag.

Travis was up.

Staring at his broad back, she relived the excitement of being in his arms. Then she remembered all the problems that awaited her with the coming of day. Fatigue assailed her, a weariness of mind more than body.

"Is it time to go?"

He swung around, his eyes catching the embers and the flames that had begun to leap along the fresh logs. "Not yet. We'll eat, then head out when the sun is up." He left the cabin.

Swinging her legs into the chilly morning air, she rose and dressed, then packed up. Keith invited them to the ranch house. Janis had breakfast ready when they arrived.

"Are you leaving today?" she asked when the four were seated at an oak table that was carved and scrolled by an expert craftsman from long ago.

Alison met her sister's eyes, which were very much like her own. The wrench in her heart was painful, a reminder of the closeness that had once existed between them.

During the night, she'd said goodbye to the children they had been. Janis was a woman, intent on living her own life and capable of making her own decisions.

Alison thanked the couple for their hospitality. She offered to leave her cell phone with them.

"I'll have the phone line in before the end of the month," Keith assured her when Janis indicated she wouldn't accept the offer.

"I'll see that the ford at the creek is cleared," Travis promised. "If the logging road is good all the way to our place, that would be a shorter drive to the highway, in case you need to get to town."

"Thank you," Janis said, sounding sincere. "I'm sure we'll be fine."

Keith didn't look quite so certain. Alison saw him exchange a glance with Travis, a telling communication between the two men that indicated an unspoken but shared thread of concern.

At last it was time to go. Donning her backpack when Travis did, Alison hesitated, then hugged her sister. Janis was stiff for a second, then she returned the hug.

"I'll be all right," she said.

"Shall I tell the parents of the situation?" Alison was compelled to ask.

"I'll call them," Janis said. "I promise. As soon as the phone line is installed."

Keith touched Alison's shoulder. "I'll see that she does."

Relieved, she nodded. "If you need anything, anything at all, please call. Janis has my cell-phone number."

"Ready?" Travis asked, standing apart from the tense family scene.

She fell into step behind him and only once did she look back. Janis and Keith walked them to the clearing, then stood arm in arm and watched as they left. There was a naturalness about the couple, as if they belonged to the rugged land and to each other.

Alison swallowed hard and faced the trail. She and her reluctant escort had miles to go before the day ended. He was keeping his distance from her. She could almost hear the buzz of an electric fence surrounding him.

Last night he'd overstepped his set boundaries. Today he was determined it wouldn't happen again. At least he didn't seem to blame her for the passion. Both knew it was a mutual thing. Her heart hammered as she recalled their kisses, then ached as she remembered his rejection.

For the next hour, they hiked steadily, down the smaller valley and into the larger one. The land began to rise as they hiked southward. To the west, she could hear the faint roar of the rapids as the Snake River plunged through the treacherous twists of the mountains on its journey to the ocean.

"We'll rest here," he said when they came to a fork in the path. "Eat some trail mix. You'll need the energy."

She propped her pack against a boulder, then sat on another one. She gazed at the scenery as she munched on the snack and tried not to worry about the future.

"Ready?" he asked.

"Yes." She slipped her arms through the straps on her pack and stood. "Didn't we miss the trail?" she wanted to know, gazing at the ridge high above them.

"No. This one joins the road that goes over the saddle and connects to our ranch. I think we can clear the weeds and get a pickup over to the Towbridge spread if we need to."

The worry returned. "I hate to leave."

He didn't reply.

"She could die, having a baby out here."

He ignored her concern.

"She's only twenty-one. Her life is just beginning."

"You're twenty-eight," he said. "Isn't it time you started living your own?"

At the harshness of his tone, she went totally still

for a second, then she calmly agreed with him. When he indicated she should follow the ruts of an old logging road, she resumed the hike, her pace much faster.

"Steady," he said behind her.

She slowed somewhat, setting an even pace she could sustain. Another hour sped by. When he called for a second rest stop, she was grateful. Although this path was much easier than going over the ridge, it wasn't a stroll through the park, either. Sinking to a handy rock, she didn't remove her pack. She was too tired.

Travis handed her his water bottle. She gulped several swallows. He gave her a bag of trail mix, then drank deeply himself. The rest wasn't nearly long enough.

"Let's go," he said after five minutes.

She started uphill. When the trail flattened out at the top of the saddle, she spoke her thoughts aloud. "I don't know her anymore. I've fed her and diapered her and even spanked her once, but my little sister is gone. It's as if I've lost some part of myself when I wasn't looking."

Travis gave her an unreadable perusal when she glanced over her shoulder. "Maybe she just grew up."

She nodded and pressed forward. The road was clearer now, less overgrown with weeds down the center. A little later, it smoothed out into a one-lane track that had been surfaced with gravel. Travis moved up beside her.

"This is Seven Devils Ranch land," he said.

She heard the note of pride in his voice. "Your land?"

"Mostly my uncle's. My brother and I are buying into it. We own almost half now."

Forty minutes later, they rounded a bend and stood on a small rise. A lovely green valley spread before them like a feast. She could see a ranch house and outbuildings, pastures and enclosures. Cattle and horses grazed in the fields. The scene was so peaceful, it seemed surreal.

"Paradise," she murmured, the ache of an unknown grief returning briefly to haunt her.

"Home," he corrected.

Another part of her that she'd been totally sure about seemed to fall away as she followed him the last mile to the charming ranch set in the pristine meadow.

Travis knew he was in for trouble when he spotted the gleam in Uncle Nick's eyes. The old man ambled off the porch where he'd been reading the paper and met them in the center of the quadrangle that separated the house from the barn and stables. "Well, who have we here?" he asked.

"Uncle Nick, this is Alison Harvey." Travis made the introductions reluctantly, the darkness shifting inside while his mood became dangerous. "My uncle," he told Alison.

"Welcome to Seven Devils Ranch," Uncle Nick

said, his gallantry putting Travis's teeth on edge. The old man still had an eye for the ladies.

He let himself look at his companion. The sun found the gold in her hair, the alabaster in her skin. Her smile was charming as she shook hands with his uncle. It didn't quite reach the depths of her eyes, though.

"Alison Harvey," Uncle Nick repeated. "Come sit on the porch. Would you like some coffee? Travis, take her backpack. We'll put her in the Rose Room."

Alison shot an alarmed glance in his direction.

"She's not staying," he told his bossy uncle.

Uncle Nick was having none of that. "Of course she is," he insisted. "Can't you see she's tired?" He chuckled as he guided Alison to the porch and nearly pushed her into a chair. "Here." He thrust her pack at Travis, then pulled another chair close and sat down.

Travis shrugged, then went inside, leaving her pack in the Rose Room that was reserved for guests and his own in his room located in the opposite wing of the house. Through the open windows, he could hear Alison speaking.

"The ranch is lovely," she was saying. "So peaceful."

"This is its best time of the year," Uncle Nick said with modest pride. "The grass is green and the trees are budding out. See those dogwoods and redbuds over there? Planted them myself more than thirty years ago."

"They're truly beautiful."

Travis had to give her credit. She sounded totally sincere with his uncle.

"So you're here to find your sister," Uncle Nick continued, changing the subject. "Did you succeed?"

Travis hurried to the rescue before his uncle could grill her in depth. "Janis is at the Towbridge place," he said, going onto the porch and closing the screen door behind him without letting it bang against the house. "The grandson, Keith Towbridge, is rebuilding the ranch."

He detailed the operation as told to him by Keith, including the war games and businessmen.

"Keith and his partner need cash flow," Alison added. "We didn't meet the partner. He's working on a lodge while Keith remodels the old ranch house."

"Which reminds me, I need Trevor to help me remove the boulders at the creek ford, then I thought we would open the back road between the two places," Travis finished the tale.

Uncle Nick gave him a shrewd glance. "Why?"

Travis tossed the conversational ball to Alison with a glance. She shook her head slightly. He raised his eyebrows at her, questioning her reticence.

"Why?" Uncle Nick repeated, his eyes on Alison.

Travis was surprised when she answered without evasion.

"My sister is living there. With Keith. She's seven months pregnant. There's no phone, no road to the house."

Uncle Nick looked shocked. ''What's that young man thinking, taking his wife—''

''They aren't married,'' Alison interrupted. She spread her hands in a helpless gesture. ''People don't think it's necessary these days.''

''That's foolish,'' Uncle Nick said sternly. ''Children need the sanctity of marriage. A family needs to be legal so everyone knows where they stand. These young people,'' he muttered in disgust, ''they don't think about the future.''

Travis had once believed that. Observing Alison nod in response to his uncle's declarations, he realized she still believed it. She wouldn't go for a casual affair.

Not that he wanted one, either. He wanted nothing to do with the woman who politely agreed with Uncle Nick as he went on and on about the importance of marriage and stability within a family.

Travis had heard this lecture. He'd been spared the details after he and Julie had married. After her death, his uncle had never brought the subject up to him again, although his brothers and cousins still got their share of advice. For all his gruffness, Uncle Nick was a dreamer. He believed in ''happily ever after.''

Restless, Travis rose and headed across to the stable. ''Is Trev out there?''

Uncle Nick nodded. ''Dinner in about an hour. Don't go off,'' he ordered. ''That's lunch to you city folk,'' he told Alison with a grin.

Travis didn't find his twin. The gelding they'd recently agreed to train as a riding horse for a neighbor was gone from the paddock. Fresh tracks indicated his twin had taken the horse out on the trail. Travis hesitated, then followed the path into the trees.

When he came to the unfinished house, set in its own woodsy clearing, he stopped. Slowly he crossed the new grass that had grown among the yellowed blades of last year's unmown lawn. Up the steps. Across the porch.

At the door, he willed the abyss to stillness as he turned the knob. The door swung open. The cold air rushed out to enclose him in a miasma of regret and grief.

He'd never understood why she'd been taken from him, how one moment could be filled with happiness and the next…with nothing.

A faint echo of laughter stirred from the blackness as fate mocked the questions that had haunted him for two years. There were no answers, just life with all its cruelties as people went through meaningless rites.

Marriage. A demand of society. Birth. A demand of nature. He wanted nothing to do with either. Reaching inside the frigid-as-a-tomb house without stepping across the threshold, he closed the door and turned his back on all that it once had meant to him.

He hadn't cleared the steps when he heard hoof-beats on the trail. Trevor and the gelding loped into view. He pulled up. "Hey, bro," he called, his glance taking in the house.

Travis leaped from the porch and crossed the small yard. "How's he doing?"

Trevor patted the horse's neck. "Super. He's a natural. He'll make a great birthday present for the guy's wife. You want to try him out?"

"Not now. I, uh, need your help with something."

Trevor swung down from the saddle. "Shoot," he said.

"Alison Harvey is at the house—"

"Here?"

"Yeah."

"You found her sister?"

Travis nodded impatiently. "She's about seven months pregnant—"

"The sister?"

"Yes, the sister. Will you listen?" He explained about the Towbridge ranch and Keith's plans, including Janis's determination to have the baby at home. He ignored the quiet flash of sympathy in his twin's eyes at the mention of a baby. It wasn't something he was going to discuss. "Anyway, we need to make sure the ford at the creek is clear. Also, the back road could be fixed with a little grading and some gravel in the low spots in case the creek floods and makes the other road impassable."

"We'd better get on it," Trevor agreed. "I don't imagine Alison is very happy about the situation."

"She's worried, but short of kidnapping her sister, there's nothing she can do."

The helplessness. That had been the worst thing.

Waiting in the hospital corridor while the doctors worked on his wife and knowing there was nothing he could do. He shoved the memory into the abyss.

"So you'll help with the road?" he finished.

"Sure. So will the rest of the family. And we can ask some guys from the neighboring ranches. Heck, we can put in a trestle bridge. Let's make a weekend out of it. Throw a big feed in, add Uncle Nick's cakes, and people will show up in droves."

He hadn't planned on anything that big, but Trevor was right. They could clear the ford in no time with help. The back road could be done in their spare time.

"Here. Ride back to the stable and see what you think of him," Trevor invited, holding out the reins.

Travis took him up on the offer. Mounted on the tall gelding, riding through the trees, he felt a return of the uncertain peace he maintained with an effort. He'd tell Alison the plans about the road. That would wipe the worry out of her eyes. She could return to her home. Then all would be well.

"Have you known my nephew long?"

Alison shook her head. Travis's uncle had been fishing for information from the moment the nephew had left them.

"He and I met last week rather unexpectedly." She explained her various attempts to get to the Towbridge ranch, making light of her forays into the wilderness, and was rewarded with chuckles from the old man.

"Here, pour up this pot of peas in that bowl and put it on the table," he said when she finished.

They were in the kitchen now, busy with the noon meal. The uncle had no qualms about putting her to work. She was grateful for the chores. It kept her from dwelling on her own problems.

"Travis is a good man," the uncle told her, giving her a shrewd glance from those heavenly blue eyes. "He's a little gun-shy with women. He's had heartbreak in his life, but he's steady as a rock."

She felt the need to clear up any question about Travis and herself. "Mr. Dalton—"

"Uncle Nick," he corrected. "Here."

When he thrust a wooden bowl filled with dinner rolls into her hands, she dutifully carried them to the table and returned. "Uncle Nick," she repeated. "Travis has been very kind in helping me find my sister, but I don't want you to…to think there's anything more."

"Don't you like him?"

"Well, yes. Of course. But—"

"You're the first woman he's looked at since his wife died. Actually the only one he's ever noticed since Julie. They were childhood sweethearts, you know. The boy's faithful. Once he gives his heart, it's forever."

"And now it's buried," she said softly, trying to be gentle because it was obvious the uncle cared deeply for the orphans who had been left in his charge.

The old man removed a roast from the oven and set it on top of the stove. "A part of him will always belong to her," he acknowledged. "He loved her with a boy's love. The man will learn to love in a different way. There'll be memories, but reality will fade until only a pleasant glow remains, the same way we recall our childhood delights."

"Can the present, with its day-to-day irritations, ever compete with those memories?" she questioned.

"Can an apple stay green and remain on the tree forever?" he retorted. "It isn't nature's way."

Giving her a disappointed frown, he moved the roast and potatoes to a huge platter and indicated she should take it to the table. She did so, beating a hasty retreat from his steely glare. Footsteps sounded on the porch. She heard Travis talking, then other voices joining in.

"Seduce him," the uncle advised as four men entered the living room and headed their way.

A jolt of shock sped along Alison's nerves. Upon meeting Travis's eyes, blood rushed to her head, making her dizzy.

Seduce him? This man who wanted nothing to do with her? This man who had resented her very presence in his mountain retreat? This man who had already loved and lost everything?

"Did you boys wash your hands?"

With nearly identical smiles—all filled with devilish amusement—the men lined up and held out their hands.

"Huh," their uncle snorted. "Travis, introduce your guest to the others, then take her to the table."

Alison resorted to the cordial smile of a politician's daughter, one that disclosed nothing of the turmoil inside.

"I'm happy to meet you," she said after Travis sorted out his twin, his older brother and his cousin for her. "You're the deputy sheriff?" she said to Zack.

He nodded.

"And you're the doctor?" she said to Beau.

"At your service." He executed a little bow and held a chair out for her at the long dining-room table.

Uncle Nick sat at the end. She was on his right with Travis beside her. Trevor, Zack and Beau sat opposite them.

"Seth sits on the other side of Travis," Trevor explained, seeing her glance at the two empty chairs. "Roni, our girl cousin, usually sits where you are." She and Seth lived in Boise and usually came up on weekends.

That left the end chair opposite their uncle unused, she noted. She thought of Uncle Nick's wife, who had died in a tragic accident, and their daughter, who was lost.

"My wife sat there," Uncle Nick said, as if reading her mind. "Tink was still in a high chair."

"I see," she murmured.

"Travis told us about your sister. We're going to fix the washout at the ford first," Trevor told her.

"I'll call everyone and invite them out tomorrow to help, then we'll have a cookout."

"You don't have to do that," she said. "I can arrange…that is, it's a county road—"

"Her father is the senator," Travis interrupted, his tone cool and without inflection. "She can get things done."

A beat of silence followed.

"Yeah, but that would take forever. Besides, we want to do it," Trevor announced, putting an end to her protests.

Alison knew when to shut up. "That's very kind of you. I'll feel much better, knowing the road is open."

"Yeah," Trevor agreed. "With your sister expecting, it needs to be done."

"Right," the other two Daltons chimed in.

Alison cast a startled glance at Travis.

"I told them." He shrugged.

The five males didn't seem at all embarrassed by her sister's condition. Alison took a deep breath. The pregnancy was a fact of life, and therefore had to be dealt with.

Grim Reality 101. She would have to tell the parents right away…before they heard it on the evening news.

"Everything is fine, Mother." Alison put as much assurance into her tone as she possibly could. "No, Janis is fine. There's a slight problem with the phone line at the ranch. As soon as it's fixed, I'm sure she'll contact you. She seems to be enjoying ranch life.''

No phone line at all was a slight problem? She hoped her mother didn't question the evasions. She hated to outright lie about the situation.

Not mentioning the pregnancy was lying by omission, her conscience reminded her.

She ignored it.

''It's been well over a week since you left,'' her mother interrupted her worried thoughts.

Anger, quick and surprising, surfaced at her mother's impatience and implied criticism. Alison bit back a retort. ''Yes, well, Janis prefers to stay at the ranch for now. Do you recall the Towbridge family?''

''There was a Dennis Towbridge who confronted your father in his early days in the senate about cattle prices.''

''It's probably the same man. Keith is his grandson. He inherited the ranch and has decided to live there. Janis met him at college.''

Okay, so she was putting a spin on how and where her sister and Keith met. She figured Janis needed all the help she could get.

''Is there something serious between Janis and the grandson?'' her mother immediately asked.

''Only Janis can answer that,'' Alison said, respecting her sister's right to tell the parents whatever she wanted them to know. ''How is Dad doing?''

''He's fine. He has a doctor's appointment Monday. Tell Janis to call as soon as possible. I have to run. Another boring luncheon of some committee.''

Alison managed a sympathetic chuckle as she said goodbye, then clicked off the cell phone and put it in her backpack. She knew her mother loved being part of the ''bigger picture,'' as she sometimes put it. Alison tried to see herself in that snapshot but couldn't.

She was suddenly tired of it all, tired and drained and infinitely sad.

Well, she had a right to be tired. She'd hiked more during the past ten days than she had the past ten years.

Sitting on the rose-patterned coverlet of the bed, she surveyed the pretty bedroom with its old-fashioned charm. Entering it had been like stepping into another era.

For a moment she sat there, her mind curiously blank, as if it, too, was tired of planning and scheming and always, *always,* considering the consequences.

A knock on the door sent her heart to her throat.

Chapter 8

"Uncle Nick says I'm to take you on a tour of the place," Trevor said when Alison opened the bedroom door. His grin was infectious.

She relaxed. "Did you draw straws and you lost?" she asked with mock sympathy.

"Heck, no. I had to arm wrestle Trav and Beau for the honor." He placed a hand over his heart to avow the truth of his statement. "Do you want to go or not?"

"That would be nice," she replied with grave formality.

Outnumbered by the Dalton gang during lunch, she'd agreed to spend the weekend at the ranch. Uncle Nick needed her help with the big cookout tomorrow night after the road repairs. Or so he said.

The final argument had been Trevor's promise that he and Travis would get with Keith and restring the telephone wires that had broken in a long-ago storm after Dennis Towbridge had died. Alison wanted to be sure the phone service was connected before she left the area.

She knew one person who would be glad to see her gone, she mused as she and Trevor ambled outside.

Travis had clammed up as the weekend plans had unfolded. If not for her duty to her family, she would have insisted on going back to the B&B that day.

She stole a glance at her handsome, easygoing companion as they walked down the front sidewalk to the road, then to the paddock where two horses chased each other along the fence. Had Travis once been as lighthearted as his twin?

Putting the question aside, she surveyed the ranch. A grand entrance formed the east side of the quadrangle defined by the ranch house, the barn and outbuildings and, to the west, an orchard enclosed in a white rail fence.

The entrance was outlined by a huge log that rested on two equally large ones. Carved into the wood was the name of the place and a date. Seven Devils Ranch, 1865. Nearby was a rail where cowboys had once tied up their horses.

Trevor leaned his arms on the top rail of the horse paddock. Alison followed suit.

"Your family has owned the ranch since 1865?"

she asked, patting one of the horses who came to the fence to check them over.

"Yeah. They came West after the Civil War."

"From where?"

"Tennessee. There wasn't a ranch here then. It was all wilderness. The first Dalton had to cut a road and build a house. The living room and kitchen are part of that original home. It burned one time, but they were able to save most of the logs and repair it."

She gazed at the one-story ranch house that had a front porch and central section made of logs. Wings extended to either side of the log part. Limestone steps that looked as if they'd been there since Stonehenge days gave access to the porch and formed the threshold under the front door.

Alison stifled the envy that rose inside her. "It's nice to know your roots," she said sincerely.

"I figure your family goes back to the Pilgrims."

She laughed. "We mostly came from starving Irish immigrants, with an Italian farmer and an indentured servant thrown into the pot."

"Was it hard growing up as a senator's daughter?"

"Not really. Sometimes it was confusing to know which home my parents meant when they talked about going home. As a child, I lived most of the year in D.C., but spent holidays and summers with my grandparents when they were alive. Later, Janis and I stayed at the family home with the housekeeper and gardener when my parents had to stay at the capital."

Beau came out of the house, waved to them, then drove off in an old pickup that had seen better days. An SUV with a sheriff's decal on the side was parked in the shade of an oak tree. Zack left in it a few minutes later.

Travis came out on the porch.

"I'm glad you came along," Trevor murmured. "My brother needs to come out of his shell. He's grieved long enough."

"You're mistaken if you think that has anything to do with me."

"Don't let him scare you away." Trevor started for the stable. "I have work to do. Get old Trav to take you for a ride up to the ridge. It's a great day for it."

The twin walked off and left her standing by the paddock. She felt like a rabbit caught too far from its bolt-hole as Travis's laser gaze settled on her. She saw his chest lift and drop as if in a resigned sigh, then he strode purposefully across the distance between them.

"You want to go for a ride?" he asked without cracking a smile.

Something perverse in her reared its head. "I'd love it," she said in the same hard tone.

He saddled up the two horses in the paddock and they rode up a limestone ridge that overlooked the snug valley. A huge rock perched on top of the bluff, looking like a table for a giant. Another rock formed a stool beside it.

"The Devil's Dining Room," Travis told her. "That's what we named these two rocks when we first came here."

"It fits, but there's only one seat. Where will the He-devil sit?"

"You're assuming the She-devil gets the stool, but I've always thought of this as his favorite place."

His eyes followed the valley from mountain peak to mountain peak, his love of the ranch reflected in the azure depths. This was his solace, she realized. The ranch and the mountains gave him whatever peace he could find.

Odd, but it did the same for her. They finished the short ride in silence, then Travis left her at the house while he went to help with the chores.

"How come her folks sent a lone female to chase after her sister?" Uncle Nick wanted to know that evening.

Travis finished setting the table. "I suppose it was because they don't have any boys."

"Seems careless of them to me."

"Yeah."

"She's a pretty little thing, but kind of quiet."

Uncle Nick, Travis recalled, had been taciturn once, but with six kids asking "why this" and "why that" during their first years on the ranch, he'd become more and more talkative. Now it was hard to shut him up when he was digging for something. Travis knew what the something was.

"She's not a candidate for marriage," he said bluntly.

"Huh. Who said she was? It would be more than any woman wanted to do to take on the likes of you boys."

Uncle Nick figured the Dalton boys had let him down in the marrying-and-having-kids department. Maybe Seth would fulfill the old man's hopes in that direction since he was the oldest of the orphans.

"How old do you think Alison is?"

"She's my age. Table's ready," he said to distract the other man.

"You can't live in grief forever," Uncle Nick said, determined to have his say.

Travis held emotion at bay while the abyss roiled within him. He was done with male-female stuff, with loving and longing and thinking life was his to command. "I'm not."

"When a man is offered a second chance, he ought to grab it with both hands." Uncle Nick removed rolls from the oven and put them in a wooden bowl lined with a napkin.

"Right," Travis said with savage control. "The way you did after Aunt Milly died."

His uncle paused, his eyes on the distant peaks visible from the window. "Love came late in life for me. It was a lovely gift, totally unexpected. For some, lightning doesn't strike twice."

Travis ignored the pain in the old man's voice even as its echo reverberated through the lonely corridors of his soul. Love was a gift made all the more cruel by being taken away. He sought the bitterness that made the loss bearable.

"It's a lonely life for a man without a woman by his side. You'll regret it when you get to be my age."

He gave his uncle a cold stare. "More than you regret the loss of your wife and child?"

"No," the older man murmured, "that's the worst pain, but a man regrets the things he didn't do, not the things he did, especially those that brought him happiness. You and Julie were happy, weren't you?"

Blue eyes met blue eyes. Travis saw the challenge in his uncle's unrelenting gaze. "You know we were," he said, his voice going hoarse, desperate as the old anguish rose once again and pressed hard against his breastbone. He didn't want to talk about this.

"Life does go on," Uncle Nick said as if to console him for all that had been taken away.

"Yeah. Tell me about it," Travis replied.

From the living room came a burst of laughter. Trevor and Alison played a battle-strategy game. Apparently she was winning.

"Tell them supper is ready," his uncle said, heading for the table with the last items.

Travis went into the living room and paused at the doorway to observe the couple who were having so much fun. He couldn't remember the last time he'd laughed like that with another person. As a memory surfaced, he quickly suppressed it. The remembrance of happy times hurt worst of all.

"She's an expert at this," Trevor grumbled, seeing him standing there watching them. He hunched over the board and concentrated on his next move.

"Dinner is ready," Travis told them. He'd heard Alison laugh several times during the game with his twin. Their merriment irritated him, and he considered punching out his brother for no reason other than his own grouchiness.

"Your house is wonderful," Alison told Uncle Nick after the four of them were seated at the table.

"The boys built most of it," his uncle said with obvious pride. "I added a couple of bedrooms when they first came here, but they redid the kitchen and the master bedroom, then added a new wing a few years ago. The living room used to be four rooms, but they took the walls out and put in bookcases and a TV. Paid for it themselves."

"I suspect Seth paid for most of it," Trevor put in. "He's the only male in this family who can hang on to a dollar long enough to get it to the bank."

"I read an article on how many people are in the stock market these days," Alison mentioned. "You'd think everyone was a billionaire, but most of them have less than ten thousand dollars invested."

"Hey, you know a lot about finance?" the twin asked.

Alison shook her head. "Actually, I have a teaching degree for business and accounting. Of course, I only taught a year before my father asked me to run his local office while he and Mother were in Washington. He found it impossible to get someone he could trust, he said.''

She stopped as she realized this sounded as if she was bragging. People who showed off were annoying.

''A family ought to help each other,'' Uncle Nick said in approving tones.

Alison relaxed under the old man's watchful eye as he urged her to eat up and put some meat on her bones. The food was plentiful and delicious. A plate of hot corn bread completed the meal.

After offering to help with the dishes and being told it was Trevor's turn to clean up, she went into the living room where Travis flicked through the news channels.

Sitting in a leather chair with a crocheted afghan folded neatly across its back, she imagined a fire in the huge fireplace and snow outside. The family would gather here and read or play games. The television—there was one on a shelf of the built-in bookcases—would be tuned in to a football game, but the sound would be muted.

''It's peaceful here,'' she began, then stopped.

Was she implying her home wasn't peaceful? She lived alone most of the time in the house her parents maintained in the state. Naturally. They had to stay in Washington.

The housekeeper and her husband, the gardener,

lived above the garage, though, so it wasn't as if she were completely alone.

There were always social functions to attend, too. And fund-raisers. She was often asked to give speeches for her father, to women's groups usually. It was a full life.

Travis glanced her way, but didn't comment.

Flames leaped in her, but his eyes were the color of distant glaciers. "All of you have the bluest eyes," she murmured, hardly aware of speaking.

Trevor entered the room. "A family trait in all the Daltons, except Seth. His mother was Native American and he got her brown eyes. Our father and uncle, another set of twins, had blue eyes. They were six years younger than Uncle Nick."

"You were lucky to have him when…when you needed someone."

Trevor nodded. "He'll soon be seventy, but I'd swear he's as strong as he was at fifty. However, he had a heart attack a few weeks ago. He's supposed to take care of himself, but he worries about us. He thinks it's his job to get us married off before he kicks the bucket."

His soft laughter touched a chord inside her and set it to vibrating. Her life had been too busy to consider marriage very often.

Doing what?

Working. Planning dinners and fund drives, answering questions and solving problems for constituents. Important things. Truly, they were. They just seemed rather distant because of other, more pressing problems at the moment.

Sighing, she let the peace of the ranch steal over her spirits. She and Trevor played two more games before bedtime while the other two men watched a documentary about water shortages in California and Florida.

Going to the pretty Rose Room, her mind filled with scenes of family life, idealistic, romantic pictures right out of Currier and Ives, with her as the center-piece.

Right. The perfect calendar heroine, that was her.

Saturday dawned bright and sunny. The morning was spent in chores on the ranch, but after a quick lunch, Alison and the twins headed for the ford where the road was washed out and where her car was parked. It hadn't once occurred to her that it might be stolen.

Her faith was justified. The car was still there, along with Travis's truck. Four other men, ranging in age from an eighteen-year-old to his father, who was in his forties, to two old school chums of the twins, were there.

They discussed the job, then unloaded a small trac-tor from the trailer behind the father's truck. With the backhoe, they stacked earth and boulders securely on each side of the creek, forming a foundation.

To her surprise, a county truck appeared at midaf-ternoon. The driver delivered two long trestles that fit perfectly on the foundation piers. "The boss says thanks for taking care of the ford. It was on our list but we had several washouts this year."

"No problem," Trevor assured the man. He explained that the Towbridge ranch had people living there again and that the road was needed. After the driver left, the workers took a break. Uncle Nick had sent cookies and sodas for them.

"Now," Trevor informed her, "if Zack will get here with the lumber, we'll have this job done."

They had hardly finished eating the last of the homemade cookies when an SUV belonging to the sheriff's department arrived. This time the driver was Zack.

"Hey, looks as if you guys need wood. The sheriff says he doesn't know anything about a delivery of lumber in a department vehicle and he doesn't want to." The older Dalton brother gave them a big grin.

"He won't hear it from me," Trevor vowed, hand on his heart. "Let's get on with it. Uncle Nick said the steaks would be ready at seven sharp."

After the cruiser was unloaded, the deputy left. With renewed energy, the men anchored the trestles, built access ramps at either end, again of packed earth and stone, then nailed two-by-four boards across the trestles.

Alison was relieved at this latter work. She'd been worried that Janis and Keith would have to drive across the trestles, keeping the tires centered on the twelve-inch-wide square logs. With the cross planks, they wouldn't have to be so precise in guiding the vehicle.

Shadows were beginning to grow long when they finished the last boards, the two work crews meeting in the middle of the bridge. Alison stretched her back. She and the older man had kept busy supplying boards to the men.

"Here," Travis said, nearly his first words of the afternoon. He handed his hammer to her. "You can nail the last one in place."

She whacked the thick nails until they were securely seated in the wood. "I feel like a VIP driving the last spike in the cross-country railroad."

"Only it was gold." Travis stored the hammer in a toolbox in the back of the ranch truck. "I think we're ready to head in."

They loaded the tractor, then formed a caravan with Trevor leading the way, her second in her car, Travis next and the neighboring ranchers last. They arrived at the Dalton place right on time. True to his word, Uncle Nick had the steaks ready when they arrived. A table on the porch was loaded with chips, baked beans, potato salad and every kind of pickle and pepper she could imagine.

Zack drove up fifteen minutes later. "Look who I found on the side of the road," he called.

With him was an older woman with ash-blond hair who turned out to be a rancher's wife and mother to the young man who had helped build the bridge. Connie Steadman also taught at the county high school.

"Uncle Nick left a message that I was to come over and have supper. I had a flat tire less than fifty feet from the house, so I called the sheriff's department to see where Zack was," Connie said, taking a seat beside her at the table. "I'm happy to meet you, Alison. Did the men get all the work done today?"

"We did," Trevor declared. "We're thinking of starting our own construction company."

"Dream on," Connie told them. "A few days of laying a road in ninety-degree heat will cure that notion. Thank goodness, we didn't go to that year-round school plan the board was considering. I want my summers free."

Alison liked the down-to-earth teacher. "I have my teaching credentials," she confided. "I only did it for a year but thought it was fun and fulfilling."

Connie's eyes lit up. "What subjects?"

"English and business."

"They need teachers at the high school. You should apply now for next year. With your credentials, you could teach accounting or any business course."

"Oh, well, I really can't. I have a job." She explained about managing her father's Boise office.

"That must be exciting," Connie said, a thoughtful look in her eyes.

"It's..." She stopped before she said "difficult." She didn't want to sound like a whiner. "It has its moments," she finished with a smile.

The meal was a happy, boisterous occasion filled

with teasing remarks about the workday. Trevor sat on the other side of Alison and kept her entertained.

She was completely at ease with him and delighted in his tales of woe, mostly caused by Connie and her fellow teachers, to hear him tell it.

Once, laughing, her eyes met those of Travis. They observed each other for a minute. Her heart began a slow, heavy beat and she was overcome with longing so intense it was painful. In that instant she knew what she wanted.

Him. As a lover. As her love.

His eyes darkened to smoldering indigo as if he read her deepest thoughts, as if he could see the longing and with it, the desire that burned bright as a new star within her. She blinked and looked away, the odd loneliness of late gathering and dimming the pleasant ambience of the cookout.

Travis Dalton wasn't for her. His heart was locked in stone as hard as the rock that formed He-Devil Mountain.

After the neighbors left, with many expressions of gratitude on her part for their help, Alison helped with the dishes. Zack headed back to town. Trevor also left to meet a couple of friends. Uncle Nick went to his room for some peace and quiet shortly after. She and Travis were left to themselves. He turned on the TV and channel surfed.

"I didn't realize a bridge could be built so fast," she said during a commercial. "Is it temporary or will it hold up to the weather for a long time?"

"It'll hold. That's why we brought the tractor out to pack the base. If the creek floods, Keith might have to make repairs. If he pursues the dude ranch idea, he may have to get the county to put in a steel frame someday."

"I see." She drummed her fingers on the chair arm. "With the phone line in, they'll be all set."

"Yeah." He flicked her a glance, then went back to surfing. "You can write up a report for your folks, then stop worrying."

"Except for the baby."

A subtle change came over him, a hardening of his features that indicated he wasn't going to discuss the child and any problems associated with it.

"It's a boy," she continued. "It seems so odd, Janny having a baby—"

He rose, spun on one foot and, bending, laid his hands on the leather arms of the chair. Surrounded by his male aura, aware of the fury in him, she waited in silence for him to speak.

"I don't want to hear about your sister and her baby," he said in a low, grating voice. "It's their problem, hers and Keith's. Let them deal with it. If they're stupid enough to live in a wilderness—"

He stopped abruptly.

"Sorry, it's none of my business," he finally muttered. Spinning about, he walked out of the house, the door slamming softly but solidly behind him.

Alison released the breath she held and with it, the pity she couldn't express. The young couple and the baby reminded him of all he'd lost. Two years ago he must have been a lot like them, sure of his life and the future.

After switching off the television, she went to the bedroom and looked through a photo album before turning out the light and settling down to sleep. The wind whispered mournfully around the house. She didn't hear Travis return before drifting off.

Chapter 9

Alison was alone in the house when she awoke. A note in the kitchen informed her that Uncle Nick and Trevor had gone to church. She wondered where Travis was. After eating a bowl of cereal, she donned her jacket and went outside.

Travis was in the paddock, riding the gelding she'd seen the previous day. From the porch, she watched him put the horse through its paces with a calm, sure touch. He didn't glance her way. When he dismounted and led the gelding into the stable, she headed toward an opening through the woods.

Yesterday she'd spied a roof among the trees. She ambled along the shaded path. Birds chirruped in happy voices all around her. Like Keith and Janis, they were busy with nests, preparing for their new broods.

She felt left out, as if all the magic of nature had passed her by. Travis Dalton wasn't *her* Prince Charming, so there would be no rites of spring for them. She managed a smile and refused to feel sorry for herself even as the intense longing surged through her.

Coming into a clearing, she stopped to peruse the house she found there. It was obviously a home, unfinished and unoccupied. She knew instinctively whose it was.

For a long time, she studied the structure, noting its clean architectural lines, the native stone on the bottom half, the cedar shingles on the top. A massive stone chimney anchored it to the ground. There were lots of windows to let in the light and frame the breathtaking views of the mountains and the sweep of the valley.

Without conscious direction, she walked across the new spring grass of the unkempt lawn and onto the porch. At the door, she paused with her hand on the knob. She feared to enter, but she knew she was going to, no matter how much it hurt to see the house Travis had built for his beloved.

With a slow turn of her wrist, the door opened and swung back on its hinges. A chill rushed out to greet her, as if the house had stored the frigid air for a long time and was eager to expel it.

With silent steps, she entered as one enters an ancient tomb, sensing its mystery deep in her bones. She could almost hear the laughter of happier days echoing through the great room and kitchen, the four bedrooms. The house had been planned for a family.

In her mind's eye, she could see them—blue-eyed boys and girls, towheaded when young as the pictures in the family album showed, their hair darkening as they grew up to take their place in the Dalton clan.

In the large kitchen, she leaned against the counter and gazed out the window at the perfect picture of woods and mountains. One by one, she erased the scenes of family life from her inner vision.

This would never be her home. Her husband would never burst through that door and swing her off her feet and kiss her breathless. She would never know the bliss of complete love and happiness acted out within these walls.

The laughter of imagined children slowly faded until there was no sound but the buzzing of a fly beating itself senseless against the window.

Those children would never be born. They wouldn't be Travis's children. His children would never be hers.

She didn't turn when footsteps sounded on the wood flooring and stopped at the archway into the kitchen.

"You here for the grand tour?" a familiar male baritone inquired, his tone shaded with sarcasm, anger and other emotions she couldn't read.

With masochistic calm, she asked, "This was the house you were building for Julie and your child?"

"Yes."

"It has the makings of a lovely home. She must have loved watching it take shape under your hands."

He made her nervous, standing there without moving, his eyes like a void, as if his soul had gone away to a place neither he nor she could reach.

"I'm sorry for invading your space," she told him. "I saw the roof from the ridge earlier and wondered about it."

The hopelessness of loving one such as him rose starkly to taunt her. But it was too late. She'd already fallen.

"Have you seen all of it?" he asked, so polite it set her teeth on edge.

"No," she lied.

He gestured for her to come with him. He then proceeded to take her from room to room, explaining the function of each as they entered, giving her an overview of the house.

"The firewood will be stored here." Travis opened a metal door next to the fireplace in the living room. "Outside, there are other doors so you can clean out ashes or replenish the logs from the storage shed I'd planned to build when the house was done."

"I see."

She was uneasy. He could tell that by her silence and the self-contained way she followed him. He didn't care. He wanted her to be apprehensive, to pay for her meddling.

He hadn't been inside this house for two years. It was the symbol of his failure as a husband. Alison should suffer for forcing him to it. He led her through the house with calculated coldness, refusing to feel anything.

"The mantel was rescued from an old house being demolished in town to make way for the new grocery. Julie liked old things like that. She refinished it, crafting the moldings with wood putty where they were broken or missing."

Alison admired the work. "She must have been very good with her hands."

"Yes, she was." He remembered soft, feminine hands touching him, stroking and exploring with an eagerness that filled him with the sweetest longing and an exquisite gentleness—

Alison pushed a tendril of hair behind her ear, and he realized he'd been staring at her hands, that it was her touch he was recalling. He blinked in confusion, then doggedly continued with the tour from hell.

Taking her arm, he led the way down the hall. "The master bedroom is back here, near the other bedrooms so we could hear the children if they woke during the night."

He was pleased at the passivity of his voice. He could almost believe he felt nothing. Stopping in the master bedroom, he pointed out the bathroom, the closets, the window seat with the built-in bookcases. The skeletal walls—wood frames without the wallboard—didn't bother him at all.

"The bedroom is on the east," he continued. "Julie wanted the light. She was a morning person and loved to watch the dawn brighten the sky.''

His guest nodded. ''So do I,'' she said.

Some part of him that watched them from a distance noted the slight quiver in her voice. He hardened himself against it. He cared for nothing.

Guiding her through the other bedrooms, the office where he'd planned to put all the ranch records on computer and the mudroom off the kitchen, which included the laundry, he told her every plan for every room, every dream he and Julie had constructed as they put each beam into place.

Finally it was done. He led the way outside through the mudroom door and around the house to the front.

''This was to be the rose garden,'' he added. ''Julie loved roses—''

Alison rounded on him. ''Stop it! Just stop it!'' she said, then put her hands over her face and turned her back to him.

He stood there, unable to move. ''It's just a house,'' he told her, edgy now that he'd pushed her beyond the brittle composure she was so good at. He realized he'd wanted to do that from the moment he'd seen the open door and realized she was inside. He'd wanted her to hurt… God, what was wrong with him?

''A house built of dreams,'' she murmured, her voice husky in a way that sent ripples along his spine.

''Dreams only half realized before they were destroyed.'' He laughed cynically. ''The house is wood and stone. Whatever it represented at one time no longer exists.''

He thrust his hand into his pocket before he did something really stupid like reach for Alison. For some reason, the visions kept getting all mixed up between the past and the present.

The sun, filtered through a hazy cloud, came out full force. Standing in the overgrown grass, looking like a wildflower in tan slacks, a pink T-shirt and nylon jacket, his companion rubbed her hands over her face, sniffed, then faced him.

He didn't like the ravaged despair he saw in her gaze or the effort it took for her to meet his eyes. He didn't like himself very much, either.

''It's okay to grieve,'' she told him. ''It's not okay to pretend dreams don't matter.''

She bent and picked the flower from a columbine, studying it as if looking for clues to one of the great mysteries of nature. The sun spun gold into her blond-brown hair as the breeze tossed it this way and that. The hunger, ever present of late, filled him with needs long denied.

''Julie wouldn't like that,'' she finished softly.

The abyss plunged and heaved. A wave of blackness rose from it, choking him with its bitterness, flaming like brimstone straight from the hell that consumed him.

With two steps, he was by her side. He grasped her shoulders, forcing his hands to a gentleness he was far from feeling. He wanted to hurt, to strike back.

"What do you, the remote, always calculating politician's daughter, know of someone like Julie?"

Her gaze was steady. "Nothing. Why don't you tell me."

The wind gusted around them and golden strands of hair blew across her face. For a second, for a terrible, terrible instant between two heartbeats, he saw another face, another pair of eyes, watching him with gentle pity—

Hearing a rustle in the clearing, he jerked his head toward the sound. A deer stood at attention at the edge of the woods, her gaze on them as if she'd just noticed the humans in her domain. Her ears twitched once, then she bounded away and out of sight.

Alison studied him, and her eyes were like those of the doe, big and soft. Sorrowful. Hurting. For him. And because of him. He didn't like causing that look. He didn't like the guilt he felt over it, either.

"Damn you," he muttered. "Why did you ever have to show up here?"

"My family," Alison began, then faltered as his touch changed, becoming gentler although he hadn't hurt her when he'd clasped her arms. His thumbs stroked her skin through the nylon jacket in an unconscious caress.

Or maybe it wasn't unconscious. A shaky breath escaped from her parted lips. His eyes went to her mouth. She almost moaned aloud when he moistened his lips.

A sense of danger became interwoven with the excitement of being near him. Her body responded eagerly, wantonly. She wanted him, desperately wanted him. It was a passion unlike any she'd ever felt.

She suddenly didn't care what was right or wrong, if they were being foolish or not. She was tired of trying to always do the right thing, of being responsible and sensible, hemmed in by loyalty and duties she resented. Yes, she resented them, she admitted, and it was like a weight being tossed aside.

Like his house, her dreams were only half-finished. She now knew what she needed to complete them.

Him.

"Alison," he said, just her name.

He said it in a raspy, shaken voice that brought all her senses to an acute edge. Tremors formed, eddied, rushed away to some far haven inside her soul.

Her name, not Julie's.

"Kiss me," she whispered, needing that from him.

He did. Thoroughly, but not gently this time. Wildly, but not callously. A shudder went through him, then he drew her closer until they touched everywhere.

There was no resisting the temptation. In his embrace she discovered the fulfillment of all her hopes.

When he slipped his hands under her T-shirt, it seemed natural to do the same to him. She loved the smooth feel of his flesh—the warmth and strength of sinewy muscles that flexed under his skin. She loved the way his taller, broader frame seemed to shelter her.

''Need to see you,'' he muttered, desperation in the words as anger faded and desire took its place.

She nodded, unable to resist the passion that raged between them. He carried her to the porch and peeled the jacket, then the top from her. Bending, he gathered her close and laid a trail of kisses down her chest to her modest white bra.

She wished she wore lace, then realized it made no difference. She'd never felt so feminine, so desirable, as she did at this moment.

He nibbled the tip of her breast, visible as a hard pebble of desire under the material.

Laying her cheek on his head, she inhaled the shampoo cleanliness of his hair and the aftershave he'd splashed on that morning. She thought of their nights together in the woods and marveled that they hadn't made love.

''I've never known passion could be like this,'' she told him, burying her fingers in the neatly cut strands. ''It almost hurts.''

''Yes.'' He drew back, his eyes so dark, they reminded her of blue-black ink. ''The call of nature is strong.''

''Overpowering.'' She wondered if she should confess that much. ''Very close to it,'' she amended.

''I wanted you from the first day I saw you hiking up the mountain. The mysterious lady of the woods,'' he named her, reminding her of their first meeting.

''Not that first day,'' she protested breathlessly.

"Yes. You tempt me more than any woman I've ever met. Why?"

It wasn't a question she could answer. His gaze roamed moodily over her as he caressed her breasts, cupping them and rubbing the sensitive tips. Little electrical currents spiraled down inside her, joining the other feelings that he incited with his masterful touch.

She wished she could have been his first love, that they could be starting on this wonderful adventure now, with no past. But that could never be.

Never, echoed the wind as it blew across them

"You're so gentle," she murmured, pressing her hands over his and fighting the sadness that haunted her.

"I don't want to hurt you." He brushed a kiss over her lips. "But it could happen. I can be...cruel."

He sighed, stirring the hair at her temple. She wished he would kiss her again.

"You confuse me. With you, I think of things I put aside long ago."

"What things?"

"Impossible ones." His smile was harsh. "Things that can never be. But I want them. And I want *you.*"

"Yes," she whispered. "You're the one thing I needed. I didn't understand before, didn't know what it was."

She now knew why she hadn't been able to marry her high-school steady or the ambitious young lawyer. It wasn't their love that was at fault. It was her own.

She'd never felt the emotion for anyone else that she now experienced for this man, this one person who spoke to her heart.

"You make me weak," he said, stroking along her throat. "You're like alabaster and stardust, radiant from within, and I have to touch you."

He ran his hands over her sides and down to her waist. He stroked her thighs and parted them. Stepping forward, he thrust gently against her. With a groan, he stripped his shirt and her bra away, so they could touch flesh to flesh.

When he pressed, she lay back on the warm planks of the porch, his body melded with hers as they half lay there in the sun. He began a slow, rhythmic movement.

Fire flowed through her veins, and she no longer was made of flesh and blood, but only of something not of this earth. As in a magical dance, she moved with him, her hips rising to the fall of his, meeting each sensual demand. The need for fulfillment made her cry out.

"Take it," he said in a ragged tone. "Take all you want. I want to feel you shake...the way I'm shaking."

She rubbed down his back and slipped her hands under his waistband until she could feel the straining muscles there as he thrust again and again. "Please. Oh, please."

Raspy cries escaped her as he took them higher and higher on passion's wings. His lips devoured hers for endless moments, then he moved to her breasts and suckled until she writhed in helpless wonder.

"It's never been like this. I've never wanted to beg," she told him desperately. "But I want more."

"Good, darling. I'll see that it's there for you."

He moved away enough to unfasten her slacks. When he stroked her intimately, every muscle in her body clenched as ecstasy rolled over her, wave after wave of pure ecstasy.

She tugged at his jeans. "Come to me."

"Can't," he said, panting heavily now. "I don't have protection."

A moan of frustration slipped from her. Then she caught her breath as he moved against her again, harder, faster, pushing her on...and on...

"But we can have this," he murmured and took her mouth in a raging kiss as their bodies strained and tensed and flexed with increasing need.

"Ohh," she cried as sweet fulfillment crashed over her. "Travis, oh, darling, yes. Yes. Yes. Yes."

He brought one thigh up over hers and pressed hard, barely moving now. She felt the ripple of his body, heard him stop breathing for a minute, then felt the long, shuddering release of his breath just before he relaxed against her.

She stroked his back and once again felt the wash of sunlight over them and heard the wind ruffling the trees.

A faint drone reached her through the wonderful lethargy. He tilted his head, listening.

"Someone's coming," he told her and pushed himself upright. He slipped his shirt on.

His eyes were dark with thoughts and feelings she couldn't read. He found her bra and quickly fastened it around her, then helped her with her T-shirt.

"I'm sorry," he began, then hesitated. "I didn't mean to do that, to go that far."

She felt the terrible hopelessness of a love that could not thrive. He wanted her, he would share his body, but his heart wasn't part of the bargain.

Tears rose from some deep well of grief, but she forced them aside. She hadn't come to the mountains expecting to find happiness, so there was no need to cry over what wasn't to be. She brushed his hair into order with fingers that trembled. "There," she said.

From the ranch house, the wind carried voices to them. Uncle Nick and Trevor had returned.

"Travis," his twin called.

"Yo," he answered. He sighed, then left her after one more searching glance.

After smoothing her hair and giving herself a second to completely regain her composure, she joined the men at the other house. They were already planning the task of checking and repairing the telephone wire to the Towbridge place.

"Why didn't the phone company repair it when it broke?" she asked.

"Ranchers have to string their own lines when they live off the public road or pay someone to do it,"

Trevor explained. "We have a spare reel on hand to make repairs, so we should be able to handle it."

"I can arrange for someone to come out," she told him. "You're taking time away from your ranch chores."

"Neighbors help out," Uncle Nick said firmly.

That ended her argument, although she was still concerned at involving them in her problems. "Thank you," she said warmly. "Since there seems to be nothing further I can do, I thought I should start home. To Boise. I can be there in a couple of hours if I leave now."

No one said anything for a moment, then Uncle Nick nodded. "If you need to go, then you should."

"I really do. I've been gone long enough."

Long enough to lose her heart, long enough to be hurt by an apology he felt he had to give. For the rest of the time she was there, she smiled and smiled until her face hurt with the effort.

Miss Braveheart. She should get a medal.

"But you'll come back for my birthday, won't you?" Uncle Nick asked. "It's on a Saturday. June eighth."

Alison didn't make any promises. It was time to go home and take up where she'd left off before that hurried trip to the Seven Devils Mountains.

"Goodbye," she said to the twins after giving the older man a hug. To Travis, she added, "Thanks for your help in locating my errant sister." She didn't look into his eyes.

"Rescuing fair damsels is our greatest calling," Trevor grandly informed her when Travis only nodded.

"Take care," Travis said, surprising her.

"Yes. Yes, I will." She hoped the other two didn't notice how flustered she became at his slight smile and the regret in his eyes, as if he apologized again for the way things were between them and the fact that he didn't, couldn't, love her.

The three men walked her outside and saw her off. She looked back and waved just before the ranch house was out of sight. Turning toward the open road, she let her gaze sweep over the soaring peaks around them. Her days of roaming through the hills and learning to be a mountain woman were at an end. She would always remember it.

However, she was returning to her rightful place, and it wasn't in this valley...or his arms.

She'd known that fact since the first night she'd slept, safe and secure, in his tent. The emptiness she'd felt of late returned with a *thud.*

Back to Grim Reality 101. Travis, while attracted to her, would never risk his heart again. He'd been too much in love the first time, too hurt by that loss.

Besides, he thought she didn't belong here. She forced herself to accept that he was probably right. It was just that she didn't feel she belonged anywhere.

Yeah, right. Poor little orphan.

She swallowed hard when she passed the city limits sign of the little town. The ache she felt was inside her. With time, she assured herself, it would heal. She turned south on Highway 55, which would take her home.

Today was Sunday, the twenty-sixth. Nearly two weeks ago, she'd arrived in town intending to find her sister and bring her home. She'd expected to be there for two days, three at the most. Instead, she'd stayed twelve.

A lot could happen to a person in that length of time. One could meet new people. Make friends. Fall in love. Be wild and foolish and miserable and happy.

One could live a lifetime, all in the space of a heart-beat.

As she'd expected, Alison found her parents in res-idence at their family home when she arrived.

"Finally you're home," her mother said, returning her hug. "I'm disappointed that Janis didn't come with you."

The familiar undertone of censure grated on Ali-son's nerves. She went to her father. "How are you?" she asked, worried that he was worse than he ap-peared.

"Fine, sweetheart. How was your trip?"

"Fine." She realized how silly that sounded in light of all that had happened.

"Your mother and I are eager to hear the details."

Alison told them of the charming town and Amelia at the bed-and-breakfast inn, about the mountain treks she'd attempted and the rescues. She described the

Dalton ranch and finished with Uncle Nick and his heroic efforts to raise six kids on his own.

She added her adventure with Merv and Harry and the war games. Finally she explained about Keith's plans for his grandfather's ranch. "Janis is helping. She was actually cooking over an open fire when I arrived."

Alison saw her parents exchange glances. Nothing would please them more than for their children to settle down with a young man from a good family. She wondered if Keith would qualify, although he didn't take part in politics.

Biting off the cynical thought, she ended the tale with a description of the Towbridge place and the repair of the creek ford by the Daltons, plus their intention of helping with the telephone line.

"They're good neighbors," her father said in approval.

"Janis promised to call as soon as the phone is working," Alison told them.

Her mother huffed in annoyance. "What happened to her cell phone?"

"Uh, she felt it was too much of an expense."

"What about college? When is she going back? She'll have to catch up on her work—"

"She isn't going back," Alison interrupted, feeling defensive on her sister's behalf. "She and Keith are, uh, in love. I think they might marry soon."

There was a beat of silence.

"What?" her mother snapped.

"She'll tell you all about it when she calls." Alison turned to her father. "When do you go to the hospital?"

He was plainly puzzled. "For what?"

"For the surgery."

"It can be done as an outpatient procedure," her mother said.

Alison was astounded. "A tumor at the base of the skull can be done without a stay in the hospital?"

"What are you talking about?" her father asked.

"The tumor," Alison said. "The one at the base of your skull. Isn't it being removed Friday?"

The elder Harvey appeared puzzled. "I'm having a mole taken off the back of my neck Friday. In the doctor's office. I won't be put to sleep or anything like that. It isn't even surgery. He'll zap it with a laser, and I'll be out in fifteen minutes."

"Oh." Alison looked at her mother.

"It could have been serious," the older woman said.

The senator chuckled. "Was that the story you used to bring Janis home? Nothing stops her once she's set on having her way."

Alison felt the sharp nip of betrayal as she realized their mother had exaggerated the situation for her own reasons, laying a guilt trip on the siblings, as Janis had guessed. Her father, blind to his wife's machinations, thought it amusing. She didn't.

Something that had been brewing in her—for a long time, she now realized—burst forth. "I have some news, too," she said, speaking to her father. "I'm resigning as your office manager. You have three other people there, any one of whom can run the place effectively."

"You can't do that," her mother protested. "Your father needs you. You know our plans for the future."

"Your plans," Alison said softly. "Your future. They aren't mine. I'm sorry, Father, but I don't want to be involved in your campaigns and political life."

The senator, looking concerned, motioned his wife to silence. "What are your plans? Do you want to go back to teaching?"

"Maybe," she said. "Maybe I'll travel for a while. Or move to California."

This last statement was a ploy to throw her family off track. She honestly didn't know at the moment where her future might lie, but a name pinged in her heart. *Seven Devils,* it whispered mischievously to her.

Her father peered at her intently. "Did something else happen on this trip that we haven't heard about?"

Alison wondered what they would say if she told them she'd fallen in love with a rancher, one who would have agreed with them about where her place was.

"This is ridiculous," her mother declared. "You can't leave when your father needs you the most."

The senator held up a hand. "Wait a minute, Virginia." He looked at Alison. "You've thought this through? You're sure this is what you want?"

She shrugged, then smiled. "I don't know what I want, only what I *don't* want. I think it's time I explored the possibilities a bit more."

Thinking of those possibilities brought a surge of trepidation...and excitement. Suddenly a whole future of possible scenarios rushed through her mind.

"Then it's settled," her father said.

"This...this delayed rebellion is irresponsible in the extreme," her mother declared indignantly.

"It's time," Alison said quietly. "Janis and I have our own dreams to fulfill."

Alison smiled at the sense of unity with her sibling. She realized her little sister didn't need her to watch out for her anymore. Alison had tried to be the family she'd thought a child needed, but Janis was on her own now, so *she* was free to go, too.

It was an odd sensation, like dropping fast in a freight elevator. For a few seconds, she was weightless and giddy with relief.

Coming back to earth, she acknowledged she would have to think carefully about where she went from here.

Uncle Nick's birthday was coming up. Maybe that would be the first stop on her journey to self-discovery.

Chapter 10

Travis sat with one hip propped on the railing of the porch and watched the sky deepen into twilight. A restless hunger ate at him. Maybe he should have gone to town with his twin. Yeah, big Friday night out—shooting pool with guys he'd known all his life.

His older brother, Zack, came out of the stable where he'd been rubbing down the gelding's sore knee. The smooth riding horse had pulled up lame that morning, but it was a simple strain, nothing serious.

Zack settled on the porch railing. "Why don't you call?"

"Who?" Travis asked, deliberately obtuse as all his defenses slammed into place.

"Alison."

The sound of her name stirred the blackness of the abyss, shifting things better left undisturbed. For a second, in the fiery red and gold of the sunset, he saw the outline of a woman, shimmering in the radiance of the sun, foolish but determined, ridiculously courageous in her quest for her sister.

A wise person looked out only for himself or herself. Maybe she would learn that someday.

"Why?" he asked, putting indifference in the word.

Zack was silent for a minute. "You could ask how her father's surgery came out."

"I already know. Someone leaked the story to the press, so it was on the six o'clock news. A mole was removed from his neck. The biopsy indicated it was benign."

"So ask about *her* health."

Travis snorted at the suggestion. There was no reason for him to contact her. She was in the setting where a politician's daughter belonged.

"If you love her, don't let her go without a fight. At least make sure she knows how you feel."

His brother's remark produced a zigzag of white-hot lightning down his backbone. He quickly checked the barriers that blocked the stupid, useless emotions and found them intact. He'd failed one woman. He wouldn't do it again.

"I don't feel anything. There was an attraction, but that's as far as it went," he admitted.

He sounded amused, casual, as if nothing mattered.

It didn't. Not to him. Alison, with her worried eyes, hadn't yet learned to let go. She took on a load of responsibility and what did it get her? Certainly not gratitude from her sister or even the thanks of her parents.

Zack didn't say a word.

"Besides, she doesn't belong here," Travis added, blocking the vision of green eyes with flecks of silver and pools of despair. She'd been tired at the time, that day he'd discovered her hiking up the mountain.

But she'd kept going, some part of him added.

And there had been that sunbeam radiance, reaching out to him, warming that cold place inside. Sunshine and fairy dust. Stuff to be admired, but not clutched to the heart and kept for all time. Nothing was forever.

"So? You're good with computers. Maybe you could find a job in the city." Without waiting for an answer, Zack ambled down the steps and over to his truck, heading for Lost Valley.

Travis waited until the blackness settled. Move to the city? He'd never considered it. He didn't now. His roots were sunk deep into the mountains. His life force, what there was of it, came from them. He'd go insane in a city.

Inside the house, the telephone rang.

Travis tensed as Uncle Nick answered. The old man talked cheerfully, chuckling and obviously enjoying himself, then he hung up. After another minute, Travis went inside.

"Anything good on TV?" he asked.

"A game show. I could've won. I knew the answer to almost every question," his uncle reported.

Uncle Nick labored over the questions as if he were the contestant with a million dollars on the line.

"Yeah, they're pretty easy," Travis agreed.

"Not all that easy."

"Who called?" The question was casual, as if he was barely interested in the answer.

"Alison."

"How was her father? Did the news get it right?"

"About the mole? Actually it was precancerous, but the doc got it in plenty of time, she said."

"That's good," Travis said, and meant it. That was one less worry for her. If ever there was a person who worried too much about others, it was her.

"She's lonely," Uncle Nick stated.

First Zack, then Uncle Nick. Travis was surrounded by worrywarts, all concerned about Alison. "Yeah? What makes you think that?"

His uncle shrugged, then surfed through the TV channels and paused at the weather. "She's given notice to quit her job managing the senator's office and is thinking about moving. She mentioned California. I don't know why she would go there."

Travis paced to the window, the restlessness hovering on a dangerous edge. Why California? Maybe she knew someone there, an old friend. Or an old lover.

"However," Uncle Nick continued, "she says she

needs to find something more fulfilling. I told her there was nothing better for a person than a home and family and honest work.''

"Yeah, so you've told us for years."

"And rightly so," the old man retorted. "A family represents the future."

Not always. Sometimes it represented failure and anguish so raw it shredded the soul. Promises made, but not kept. He walked out of the living room, heading for his bedroom and solitude.

An elusive golden brightness seemed to dance down the hall in front of him, always out of reach. He realized it was moonlight shining in the far window.

"Something needs to be done," he heard his uncle mutter before he closed the door.

Lying on the bed, his thoughts went to Alison and her courage, her deep loyalty, which he doubted her family deserved, and her sense of duty. She'd been annoying, she'd driven him mad with her persistence, but she hadn't flinched or wavered in her goal.

Yeah, and she'd been hurt for her efforts, first by her sister's angry reception and then by her parents' careless manipulation when she'd realized they'd sent her on a wild-goose chase under the pretense of serious illness.

No one deserved to be used like that. The anger churned in him as he imagined her glow diminished, her smile subdued but bravely in place as her sharp mind put all the pieces together. Alison, who'd believed everyone was as honorable as she was, had apparently had the scales stripped from her eyes, thus her decision to find a new life.

Something in him twisted painfully. He shoved the pity under the inky surface. Live long enough and everyone learned that life was treacherous. A person had to be on guard every moment.

After a while, he rose and prepared for bed. He'd had a long day and tomorrow would be no different. Slipping between the cool sheets, he tried to relax and induce sleep. Instead, he recalled sleeping in a tent with a woman nestled against his side as she sought his warmth.

Her hair, even in the darkness, had shimmered like spun gold, and he hadn't been able to resist touching it…touching her. She'd been silk and honey in his arms, the embodiment of fantasies he'd thought long dead and buried in the black chasm that was his soul.

Not again, he vowed. He wasn't sure what he felt for Alison, but he wouldn't be sucked into the happily-ever-after thing. Love? Yeah, he'd been there. It was the closest thing to hell he'd ever known.

The void roiled and split apart, spewing a lava flow of need and desire throughout his body. Gritting his teeth, he wondered what sins, from what past lives, he was now paying for.

Alison signed her name to the last form. She placed it on top of the other forms and slid them into the waiting envelope. There. Finished.

It was Friday, June the seventh. Now she only had to wait about six weeks to see if she had a job replacing a pregnant teacher who wouldn't return come autumn.

Fear nibbled at her. She paused, her hand hovering over the trash can. The teaching job was at the county high school twenty-five miles from Lost Valley.

What would Travis think if she moved there?

Some philosopher had once said people wouldn't worry nearly so much about what other people thought of them if they realized how seldom others did.

She'd been home almost two weeks and hadn't heard a word from anyone on the Dalton ranch, except for last week when she'd taken her courage in hand and called. Then she'd spoken to Uncle Nick and told him about her father and, very briefly, about her plans to go back into teaching, maybe with a move to California thrown in.

Uncle Nick had informed her they needed teachers in the county, his manner sharp with disapproval that she would consider leaving the state. He'd also been disappointed when she'd explained she had work to do and wouldn't be coming up for his birthday party. She'd mailed him a present earlier in the week.

Affection for the old man soothed her unruly emotions. She sighed again, irritated with herself for the unsettled feelings that plagued her. She wasn't one of those females who reacted hysterically to every little thing. She was cool and in control, a thinking person.

As if to give lie to her self-discipline, she fought the need to put her head down on her desk and cry...just cry. But of course she didn't.

She placed stamps on the manila envelope and put it in the mail bin.

It was late afternoon and she was alone in the office. She'd agreed to continue to work for her father until she got a new job. Her mother was angry with her, her father absentminded about her resignation, as if it hadn't yet impinged on his conscious mind.

Her sister had called and managed to win forgiveness for her disappearance. No mention had been made of the coming baby. No promises had been given to return home.

Alison wondered if they were a strange family or basically like the rest of the world. Hearing footsteps in the hall, she stopped the morose musing and got busy.

Retrieving her purse and suit jacket, she locked the office and headed for the elevator. A man stepped from an adjoining corridor, blocking her way. Her heart knocked against her ribs.

Beau took her arm. "This is an abduction," he told her. "Will you come peacefully or do I have to use force?" He gave her a reassuring grin.

"I hope you're talking about dinner," she told him, calming down. "I haven't eaten in hours."

"Well, no," he said, his manner serious and a bit worried. "I'm talking about a trip."

Worry set in. "Where?"

"Home."

"Home?" she asked, confused.

"Consider this a vacation. Hurry," he advised. "It's getting late."

The Dalton cousin ushered her into his old pickup.

"I shouldn't do this," she said as they left town.

"You have no choice. Besides, it would hurt Uncle Nick's feelings if you missed his birthday party."

She told him the reasons she couldn't go to the ranch. He listened and nodded and kept driving.

After two hours on the road and a quick meal, she was surprised again when they turned off a side road before reaching the ranch house. She heard the soft whickers of horses as Beau stopped, and surmised they were heading for a more remote area.

There could only be one reason for this absurd abduction. Her heart drew into a knot as she thought of what it could be.

"Trev?" Beau called.

"Here," a masculine voice answered.

Beau opened the camper on the back of his pickup and pulled out a nylon bag. "You might want to change into something more comfortable."

"What is this?" she demanded, finding new jeans, two T-shirts, pajamas and toiletries inside.

"Clothes. So you can ride."

There were also socks and sneakers in the duffel bag. She put on the shoes after slipping into casual clothing and tying her jacket around her waist.

Her heart began a tom-tom beat. She'd planned on

returning to Lost Valley if the teaching job came through. However, she wasn't sure her courage was up to facing anyone tonight.

Dressed, she called to the cousins. "I'm ready."

Trevor was already mounted when she stepped from behind the truck. Beau gave her a leg up on a tall gelding, then handed the duffel to his cousin.

"Any trouble?" he asked.

"No," Trevor said. "Everything's ready. Come with me," he told her. With a wave to Beau, the twin escorted her up a winding trail and down a sharp ridge.

Twenty minutes later, he announced, "This is it." He gestured in front of them and moved aside to let her see.

The sun was setting beyond a spectacular view of the peaks to the west, bathing the remote cabin in golden light.

On a rise to the southeast, she recognized the outcropping the Daltons called the Devil's Dining Room. The logging road she and Travis had hiked from the Towbridge ranch was nearby. They were no more than an hour or so from the Dalton house by foot, she realized.

"I can't believe you're doing this," Alison said for the tenth or twentieth time.

When she'd realized Beau really intended to take her to the mountains, her heart had flipped several times in dread, anticipation and so many other emotions that she'd lost count. All her arguments about why she couldn't go on this wild-goose chase had fallen on deaf ears. Beau had assured her it was "all planned."

"Dismount," Trevor ordered.

He slid off his horse and reached for her. Alison pulled free of the stirrups and let him help her down. Taking the gelding's reins, Trevor mounted again and turned back toward the trail. He dropped the duffel at her feet.

"Wait!" she cried. "When will you be back?"

"Tomorrow," Trevor said. "That should be enough time."

"Enough time for what?" she asked to detain him. She knew this was a kind but foolish idea on his part.

"Go to the cabin," Trevor advised. "There's food and, um, other things for you there."

He rode off, leaving her standing in the soft hues of twilight. Little bolts of lightning ran over her nerves as she slowly turned and stared at the wooden cabin. She had to go in sometime. Picking up the luggage and pushing her purse strap back on her shoulder, she headed for the shelter.

The door had a padlock on it, the key in the lock, but she found it wasn't snapped closed. She removed the padlock from the hasp and turned the rusty knob. The door swung open on squeaky hinges.

"Ohhh," she said in alarm as a tall muscled figure leaped from the dark interior.

The flying tackle took them both to the ground, then the world spun in confusion as they rolled, ending with her on top of a lanky, tough body primed for a fight.

"Travis," she murmured.

"Are you okay?" he asked in a near growl. "I thought Trevor had returned. I was going to kill him."

"He left. How long have you been locked in?"

"Long enough to contemplate murder."

She nodded. "Beau kidnapped me when I left the office after work."

"Beau was in on it?" He cursed, then seemed to notice their position. "Would you mind moving? There's a rock digging into the middle of my back."

Hastily she moved off the warm masculine body cushioning her from the ground and gathered the duffel, purse and jacket that had fallen during the brief tussle.

With an angry glance in the direction she had come, Travis bowed from the waist and gestured at the door of the cabin. "Welcome to my humble abode."

She went inside. A single twin bed, with a pillow and sheet already on the mattress and several blankets folded at the end, graced one wall. A woodstove stood near the other. In the middle was a card table and four chairs of the foldable variety.

Shelves were stocked with cereal, powdered-milk boxes, oatmeal, canned vegetables, meats and stews. There were fresh five-pound bags of flour and sugar, a big can of coffee and a loaf of bread along with two mesh bags, one of oranges, one of apples. A case

of bottled water, a box of breakfast tea and a bag of
energy bars finished off the loot. A lantern had been
provided, along with plenty of fuel, matches and firewood.

The place had electricity. A single light with a
dingy shade was attached to one wall.

"All the comforts of home," she said after a quick
glance around. "What is this place?"

"An emergency cabin in case someone's caught in
a storm. Did my cork-brained brother happen to mention how long he planned to keep us here?" Travis
asked, disgust rampant in his tone, fury in his stance.

"Uh, overnight, I believe. Uncle Nick's birthday
dinner is tomorrow."

Travis cursed expressively but with less descriptive
terms than if she hadn't been present, she suspected.
She couldn't help it. She smiled.

Travis's fury dried up like a puddle in sunlight.
Alison's smile was a beacon on a dark shore, steady
and bright. But then, he'd known she was like that,
always ready to make the best of a bad situation.

"You don't seem upset," he said. "Were you in
on the plot with them?"

She shook her head. "I'm merely stunned."

"This is so typically Trevor." His snort of laughter
wasn't amused. "The whole bunch think they know
what's best for me."

He stood at the open door and studied the terrain.
The mountain air was cooling rapidly as the day faded
into the purple shades of evening.

Alison suppressed a shiver and let her eyes roam over him, taking in the attractive masculinity, the strength she recalled each night in her dreams.

The slam of the door brought her back to reality. "There's a storm brewing," he said. "We'll have to stay put tonight."

It hadn't occurred to her that they would try to leave. "Yes, I thought so."

He checked the woodstove. Finding starter, kindling and logs already laid, he put a match to it. In a few minutes, the cabin began to warm. He added water to the teakettle and put it on the stove.

"Have you eaten?" he asked.

"Uh, yes. We stopped on the road."

He studied the pantry shelves. He went still, then cursed again under his breath. Finally he opened a can of beef stew and one of vegetable soup, mixed them in a pan and set it next to the kettle. When the food was ready, he poured up a bowl, glanced at her, then fixed another.

"Join me. This will warm you up."

She went to the table while he set out a tin of crackers. The meal passed in complete silence.

"Thank you," she said. "I do feel better. Warmer," she added at his quick glance.

He washed the dishes in a pan of soapy water. She dried and put them away. She made two cups of hot tea and handed him one, then pulled a chair close to the stove. He added several logs and joined her.

And there they sat while the wind whispered outside the cabin and the tension built inside. She'd never felt so awkward and uncertain. The barrier around him sizzled like a high-voltage fence.

But when she met his eyes, she knew it wasn't an impenetrable wall. Passion had already breached his defenses. A sensation like lightning zigzagged through her, hot and wildly out of control. She looked away, but the feeling didn't fade. It grew with each moment until she thought she would burst with longing.

"We need to get some sleep if we're going to get out of here early in the morning," he announced in a flat voice. "You can have the bunk. I'll take the floor."

"Oh, no, I couldn't," she protested. "I don't mind sleeping on the floor. I—I like a hard bed."

He laughed at her stumbling lie. From a chest under the shelves, he removed two more blankets, spread one on the floor between the stove and back wall, then removed his boots and stretched out with the other blanket over him.

Rolling over so his back was to the room, he said, "Turn out the light when you're ready."

After brushing her teeth using only half a glass of water and turning out the light, she went to the bed and slipped out of her shoes, then glanced at her jeans and shirt. She'd sleep in those. With two blankets over her—there was only a bottom sheet—she snuggled down to wait out the long night. She wondered if she should warn Travis that she talked in her sleep. Oh, but he knew that.

The wind picked up, then the rain started. At first the storm was full of lightning and thunder, then it gentled into the patter of raindrops on the metal roof. The sound lulled her into sleep.

"Wake up. Alison, wake up. You're dreaming."

She sat up abruptly, smacking her head on Travis's chin. His hand slipped from her shoulder and bumped against her breast. Her nipple peaked at once.

They both froze, then jerked back at the same time.

"I must have been talking in my sleep." She laughed nervously, aware of his nearness in every fiber.

"You sounded distressed," he told her, his voice low, a lullaby that calmed the fears of the dream.

"I was lost in the mountains," she explained. "And I was expecting. Twins, I think. I needed a safe place. There was a cave but I was afraid to go in. It was the only refuge from the storm. I knew there was great danger in there, but I didn't know what it was, and I didn't know what else to do. It was so real."

In the faint light from the stove, she saw his chest lift and fall in a deep breath. The rain continued outside. She noticed the temperature had dropped.

He moved away without saying anything. Pulling the blankets up to her chin, she watched as he built the fire back up. Instead of lying down, he wrapped a blanket around his shoulders and settled in a chair.

He looked so very alone.

"I'm sorry I woke you," she said hoarsely. She cleared her throat.

He turned his head until he could see her. She couldn't turn away, although she knew she should. She should pretend to sleep until this moment passed. She didn't.

They continued to observe each other as the wind whispered seductively around the cabin and the rain pattered on the roof. The glow from the fire glimmered through the isinglass window of the stove, casting a rich warm ambience about the room.

He rose. The blanket fell to the chair.

Her breath knotted in her throat and she didn't take another until he stood by the bed again.

"Tell me no," he said, the words raw as if it hurt to say them.

Chapter 11

Alison propped herself on an elbow. "No," she said, but it was a denial of the request, not the person, and they both knew it.

When he bent to her, she met him halfway. Closing her arms around his shoulders, she clung to him as the last terrifying shreds of her dream faded.

Safe, she thought. Safe at last. In his arms she'd found her haven. She knew it was temporary.

He sat beside her and lifted her to his lap. With his back braced against the wall, he cradled her against him, just holding her, as if reluctant to take the next step.

"Your touch is gentle, cherishing," she whispered.

He bent close. "I don't feel that way. I want to ravish you right here, right now."

The words were savage, filled with rage and a haunting despair, but she wasn't afraid, not of him. Maybe herself, though. "I want you, too."

Desperately. Wildly.

"Like this?" He grabbed a handful of her hair, closing his fist on it and squeezing hard, but careful not to pull. "Like I want you? The demand of the body? A physical thing?"

"Yes." That wasn't all she wanted from him, but she couldn't tell him that. He wasn't ready for confessions of undying love, not while every muscle in his body screamed with tension that said he wanted to resist the need and hunger that arced between them. "I'm sorry," she whispered. "I'm sorry you were hurt."

A breath hissed between his teeth. He closed his eyes as if in pain. She hurt, too, with longings so strong she knew she wouldn't deny them tonight.

A clap of thunder directly over the cabin made her jump. She wondered what had been hit. Maybe her. Maybe her heart had been struck and was lying in pieces inside her.

"It's only thunder," he said, running soothing hands over her arms. "A summer storm in the mountains."

"In me, too," she admitted. "A storm in me."

He studied her for a long second, then, "And me," he murmured. "Everywhere."

Resting an arm over her drawn-up knees, Travis

leaned forward and touched her mouth with his, a glancing kiss, not nearly enough to satisfy.

"I'm not this way," she said suddenly. "I'm always in control. I never get rattled. Or do foolish things."

He moved, sliding his hands up her sides until his thumbs rested under her breasts. He could feel her heart beating in rhythm with his, sense the worry in her. She always worried. "Until now."

Leaning his head against hers, he tried to still the pound of hot blood through his body. He wasn't convinced she was ready for this...for sex, nothing more.

She moved, then her hands caressed his shoulders and down his chest, bringing a gasp that shuddered all the way through him. Her touch was bliss. Too much bliss. He had to be careful. A man always had to be careful.

When she lowered her knees and slid down on the bunk, he followed so that they lay side by side, touching lips and bellies and thighs, arms and legs all entangled. The hunger increased to a roar that drowned the storm.

"You're like silk and velvet, the finest things I can imagine," he said as he caressed under the shirt she wore. Her skin was warm and he remembered the radiance that seemed to come from inside her. He needed that...no, it was a physical thing. That's all he wanted.

Her smile erased the worry in her eyes. "You, too,

but solid. Like earth. Like rocks and trees and wild things.''

''I'm wild for you,'' he said, ''but you can tell that.''

Those words were okay. He wasn't making promises. He didn't have to cherish or protect, except for one thing. His twin had thoughtfully included protection in the supplies, so they were okay there.

Pulling his head to hers, Alison kissed him with all the longing that had stayed hidden inside her, with the thirst of unquenched passion and the sweetness of dreams she'd thought were lost.

She was trembling.

So was he.

He branded her with kisses.

She gave each one back and with them, the pieces of her heart, one at a time until he possessed the whole.

Like metal to magnet, he lowered his head and touched her mouth. And then she was lost, truly lost.

Reason dissolved like snowflakes in the heat of their passion. His kisses drove her beyond thinking. For once in her life, she felt this was truly her.

Vaguely she realized the feelings had been there a long time, but like Sleeping Beauty, desire had lain dormant until the right prince came along.

But maybe he wasn't her prince. He had made it clear she wasn't his princess. She shoved the thought aside as despair dimmed the moment.

She said his name. There was more she wanted to

say, but a lifetime of repressing her deepest longings
came to her aid. She wouldn't burden the magical
moment with demands, wouldn't ask for more than
the moment.

He shifted slightly so that their bodies meshed
chest to chest, thigh merged to thigh. She found it
wasn't enough.

Stretching upward, she arched into his strong, masculine frame and felt the kick of his heart against her
breast. Her pulse pounded, too.

"Easy," he murmured, kissing her ear, her throat.
"There's time, all the time we want."

"I need you...your strength, your tenderness."

Cupping her face in his big hands, he gazed deeply
into her eyes. "With you, I want to be as gentle as
possible. But I feel fierce inside. Like a warrior. I
want to conquer, to claim the prize—you."

"It's the same with me," she admitted.

Burning with needs she barely understood, she ran
her hands along his back and under his shirt so she
could touch his warm, living flesh. It seemed so natural to press against him and let her body experience
the feel of his.

When his hands moved between them, she closed
her eyes and leaned her head against the pillow.

"You are incredibly beautiful," he whispered, lifting her shirt and pushing the material up her chest.
"Like sunlight. Like fairy dust."

She saw that, in the firelight, their bodies indeed
glowed like molten gold.

In a second, he had the bra unfastened and pushed upward. He took her breasts into his hands and pressed his face between them, turning so that he could kiss one then the other. Flames erupted at each spot he touched.

She caressed his hair, his neck, the long line of his spine, the slender length of his hips and thighs. Finally, emboldened by passion, she touched the front of his jeans.

He sucked in a harsh breath.

Leaning her head back, she stared into his eyes, not bothering to hide the hunger as she rubbed slowly up and down his body. He opened her jeans and hooked his thumbs under the waistband.

Travis waited for her to come to her senses and refuse further involvement. He steeled himself for it, to let her go as he knew he should.

But there was no denial in the smile that lifted the corners of her mouth or in the darkness of her eyes, dilated with the passion they couldn't deny.

"Yes," she said, barely audible.

His heart nearly leaped out of his chest. Tomorrow, either or both of them might regret this moment, but for now…for now…

When he sat up and began removing his clothing, she did the same. When she pushed his shirt off his shoulders, he did the same with hers.

"Have to touch you," he said, drawing her close. "You make me ache in ways I've never ached before."

"I know. It's the same for me. I don't understand why or how."

"It just is," he whispered against her lips, nipping at them in tender forays. "Like needing air and water and food. Like living. You bring me to life."

Alison closed her eyes as desire ricocheted through her, mixed with the pain of future loss. "The time passes so fast."

"Too fast," he agreed, leaving wildfires on her skin as he kissed along her neck and collarbone.

Then he wrapped her close and settled against the blankets, his body stretched out, partially covering hers. She opened her thighs and he slid one leg between them. Outside, the storm flashed and roared; inside, the heat of a thousand suns burned between them.

Aeons later, she slipped her hands between them and stroked him intimately. He lifted his head and watched her for a solemn minute. "More?" he questioned.

"More."

He bent and kissed her mouth with such tenderness she nearly wept. She trembled uncontrollably.

"I won't hurt you," he assured her when she stared at his beautiful masculine body, fascinated by the differences between them.

"I know. I'm not worried." She was breathless. "It's just that I want you so." She broke off, not sure she wanted to disclose this much.

He expelled a harsh breath. "Maybe you shouldn't be so honest."

Travis gazed into her eyes and had a sudden insight into a life crammed with appointments, of every moment scheduled and accounted for, of duty beyond her years.

"When did you have time to dream?" he asked, sorry for that young girl, and didn't give her time to answer.

He explored every nook and cranny of her exquisitely feminine body. She wasn't inhibited, he discovered. Instead, she followed his lead, intensely interested in every sensation and caress they could share. After thirty minutes of such exploration, he was near bursting.

"Ready for more?" he asked, his lips against her ear.

"Y-yes."

He didn't miss the slight quaver. Extricating himself from their embrace, he retrieved a condom from the box on the shelf. Her eyes widened slightly.

"Trev thought of everything."

"I'm glad. I don't want to wait. I don't think I could stand another night without you, without knowing—"

"How it could be between us," he ended the thought for her. "I've thought about it, too."

He finished his task, then kissed her again, his tongue enticing her into honeyed play with his. Then his hands roamed slowly down, past her waist, circling her belly button and settling intimately at the juncture of her legs.

Alison tried to relax but she was acutely aware of every place he caressed as he made his way down her body. She clutched his hips as he swung over her, both his legs now between hers. Like a full-body massage, he caressed all of her by sliding his body up and down hers. It was wildly satisfying and pleasing.

"More," she said as tension rose even higher.

"Anything the lady wants," he told her, his tone passionate and thrilling to her ears. "I would do anything to please you."

"You do please me…when you touch me…when we kiss. It's so perfect."

He gazed at her breasts. "You're perfect, the most perfect woman I've ever seen."

Then he joined them into one.

His pleasure increased hers in ways she'd never imagined. She'd never shared such heated kisses, never given this much of herself, never taken so much delight in simply touching. When he caressed her intimately, she writhed against him, wanting fulfillment.

"When you touch me…" She didn't know how to say all he made her feel.

"Me, too," he whispered. "It's the same when you touch me. I lose my mind."

"Yes. Oh, yes." Then she laughed because she wanted the insanity and the mindless joy of the moment. She wanted this man and no other. And in that moment of crushing happiness, while stars burst around and within her, she knew she wanted him forever, even if it could never be.

Travis was aware of Alison in a way he'd never been aware of another person. He knew where she was in her passion and how close she was to the edge. He moved against her, letting her experience the full caress of his body on hers. She went very still, then she trembled all over and held on to him as she cried out softly again and again.

He couldn't wait another second. He claimed the prize he'd wanted nearly from the moment he'd spotted her on the mountain trail. Triumph burst through him in a bright rainbow of color as he closed his eyes and let the hunger take him until he was completely sated.

"Ahh," he said on a low moan as he sank against her, unable to move at that moment.

When she opened her eyes, the radiance was there, a gentle sun pouring forth from her inner self.

Alarm spread through him. Fate had a way of extinguishing the brightest flame, and he wanted no part in that. He didn't want to be around when that shimmering brightness dimmed and flickered out.

He rolled to the side. She closed her eyes and soon fell asleep. Lying beside her, he breathed deeply, pulling her sweet scent inside him like a balm. Staring through the rafters to the slanted angle of the roof, he remembered something Uncle Nick had once said.

"A man must build his home big enough and

strong enough to hold all the treasures the woman will bring to it,'' the wise old uncle had told his wards.

For the first time, Travis understood what that meant. Holding Alison in his arms, he'd caught a glimpse of the bounty that a woman could bring to a man. He wondered what a man who had nothing inside to give could bring to a woman.

Still pondering this odd question, he fell asleep, his body cupped around hers, his slumber deep and quiet and content for the first time in two years.

Travis woke Alison at first light. ''All good things come to an end,'' he said, trying for a light note. ''It's almost dawn. We'd better go.''

The fire had gone out, so they ate a cold breakfast and decided to forgo coffee. Travis gave her a bottle of water and an energy bar and kept the same for himself. He tied a rope through the handles on her duffel and attached it to the day pack he'd brought, then slipped the straps of the pack over his shoulders. ''Let's go.''

Outside, he found the wooden shutters had been nailed closed, which was why he hadn't been able to open them from the inside. A hammer had thoughtfully been left on a stump below one of them.

The freshly stocked pantry should have been his first clue to his twin's intent. He'd been furious when he realized he'd been tricked into going to the cabin for a supposed fishing trip. Trevor had planned this to the last detail, including securing the windows before locking him inside…and the box of condoms he spotted while he prepared their supper.

The fury was gone, along with the mindless passion. Now he felt only a bone-deep weariness, as if he'd fought his way through a dangerous quagmire during the dark hours. Glancing at his companion, he noted her composure. It was the face she showed the world, not that of the woman he'd held last night.

From the trees came the sleepy calling of birds as they woke to the new morn. He studied the clouds to the south of them. That was a worry. A new squall was heading their way.

Indicating she was to follow, he started out. She fell into step behind him without a murmur.

He tried not to recall the passion of the night. Trevor and Beau had meant for him and Alison to spend the night at the cabin. They would be elated that their plan worked. But what now?

Glancing over his shoulder, he was rewarded with a smile from her, this golden woman with the sun-kissed radiance that upset the safety of the darkness inside him, making him want to reach out and grasp that warmth.

It wasn't going to happen. He had nothing of value to offer someone like her. He knew that even if she didn't. She deserved the best…a first love…an intact heart, not pieces…a future…

"I'll shoot my brother on sight," he promised grimly.

"Uncle Nick wouldn't permit it."

Her manner was amused, but he detected the quietness beneath the calm she projected. The abyss bubbled and boiled as he sensed things between them better left alone.

"You're right. I'll have to beat him up when I catch him alone. You can help," he responded flippantly.

Her soft laughter winged its way right down to the innermost part of him. There were no recriminations in either her eyes or her smile.

He could offer her his body. The passion was enough for him, but someplace inside her were dreams that needed to be fulfilled. He couldn't do that for her.

"I'm sorry about all this. I don't know what Trevor was thinking, but Beau usually has better sense."

"It was rather fun, being kidnapped and abandoned in the wilderness. I feel like a real mountain woman."

The stoic cheer caused an ache inside him. He examined his feelings—the odd tenderness, induced by her humor at the situation; the hunger that wasn't yet appeased; the ache beneath his breastbone, caused by her shimmering warmth and undaunted valor. This wasn't good.

They fell into a rhythm, him ahead, her behind and matching his stride with three steps to his two. The climb to the logging road wasn't long, but it was steep. He heard her panting when they stepped onto the gravel. "We'll take a breather."

"The road has been graded," she noted, scuffing a toe over the fresh surface.

"Yeah. Trev and I worked on it and added gravel. Keith can get to the county road from two directions." He paused, then asked, "Did your sister call?"

"Yes, however she didn't mention the baby." She sighed, then added, "Thank you for all your help."

"It was nothing one neighbor wouldn't do for another," he said before she could go all gushy with gratitude the way women did. He hurried on, walking beside her.

They proceeded up the road that climbed a long ridge bordered by trees on one side and a cliff on the other. He slowed his pace when he heard her breathing in quick gasps.

Peering at the darkening sky, he could see more clouds blowing up rapidly toward them.

"You have a jacket?" he asked.

"Yes, in the duffel."

He stopped and retrieved both their jackets. "New clouds are moving up from the south."

A moment ago, he'd heard the rumble of thunder and felt the first chill breeze from the new squall caress his face.

"It's going to pour," he warned. "Do you have your cell phone?"

"Yes, in my purse."

"We'll try the house from here. If we can reach Uncle Nick, he'll come pick us up." He tried the call but got nowhere. "Too many mountains," he grumbled, handing the phone back.

For a second their eyes held as memories of their previous nights in the mountains arced between them.

Then it was back to hiking. He went faster as the thunder rumbled again and again, closer and closer. He thought of chills, pneumonia, human frailty.

A light rain started a couple of minutes later. He checked his watch. Probably another forty minutes of hard walking before they reached the ranch house.

The little creek beside the road rushed downward with increasing volume. Travis studied it. Heavy rain was falling on the higher elevations and heading their way. The jackets offered minimal protection.

"Is something wrong?" she asked.

He didn't want her to worry, but he had to tell her the truth. "The storm is growing worse. The only shelter between here and the ranch is a tree. We'd better keep moving."

A flash lit the sky, and a finger of lightning hit a dead tree on the ridge high above them. The tree sizzled brightly for a minute, then the flames were extinguished by the rain. Travis blinked, dazzled by the brilliant display.

"I'm glad we aren't on the ridge trail," Alison said.

"Yeah. We'd be barbecue about now."

Her smile flashed. He wished she would complain. Somehow it would make things easier, if only she wasn't so damn stoic. But she was, and he had to live with it.

"Let's go." He headed on up the road at a brisk pace, slowing only when he heard her running to catch up. "After the next hill, we'll be on the downward slope."

"Good."

Head down against the wind, they kept going as the rain became a downpour. "We should have stayed at the cabin," he said at one point.

"We couldn't."

"Why not?" He didn't mean to snarl, but he did.

She glanced once at him, then away. "Because we would have made love again, and you don't want that."

It took him a second to collect his thoughts after that bombshell. "Do you?" he demanded savagely, his heart thumping while the void inside whirled and heaved.

"Well, yes, I think I do." She held up a hand as if to forestall his anger. "I know you don't want involvement and that you wish I'd never shown up here, but life happens. I can't change that."

He cursed silently, but it did no good. He stopped. So did she. "Sometimes you drive me crazy," he muttered, then he reached for her.

Her lips were sweet and supple against his. She wrapped her arms around him, returning his embrace with a show of open desire that burned clear through him.

Standing there in the rain, a chill wind blowing down his collar, he was suddenly warm, as if he held the radiant heat of summer in his arms. What did the future matter when he could have this moment, when they could share the most elemental of human needs.

Moving her head, she murmured something.

"What?" he said, letting his lips roam over her damp face until he found the protected place beneath her ear where her skin was dry and her perfume lingered in an enticing whiff of floral nectar.

"I think someone is coming," she repeated.

He paused, then the words sank in. Glancing down the road, he saw twin lights stabbing through the dim morning light, coming at a pace that was just short of dangerous.

"Something's wrong," she said.

He'd just reached the same conclusion. He shuddered as a trickle of cold rain seeped down his neck.

Chapter 12

Travis waved at the approaching vehicle. Alison was relieved when the SUV stopped, blinding her in the glare of its headlights.

"Dalton?" Keith Towbridge called out.

"Yeah, Travis," her companion said, automatically supplying his name so the neighbor would know which twin he was. "Let's get inside," he said to her.

Guiding her in front of him, he opened the SUV's front passenger door and lifted her into the seat, then he got into the back seat and slammed the door against the rain.

"Thank God," Keith said. "I was on my way to your place. We need help."

"What kind of he—" Travis began.

A moan sounded from the rear of the vehicle. Alison jerked around, her heart lodging in her throat. She knew instinctively who was in pain…and why.

"Janis," she said. "She's in labor?"

"Yes," Keith told them grimly. "I don't think we're going to make it. Her water broke. It happened all of a sudden. We're supposed to start classes next week," he finished, as if this fact would delay the inevitable.

"Ali?" came a faint call from the back.

Alison climbed over the front seat and peered into the cargo space. In the pale light, she saw Janis lying on a sleeping bag, her hands clenched in its folds. A pillow and blanket lay close by and towels were placed under her.

For a second, Alison felt faint. She turned to Travis, hating to ask but having no choice. "Do you know anything about delivering a baby?"

The bones seemed to stand out against his skin, giving him a harsh, foreboding countenance as he hesitated, then he nodded. "I've had some training." He removed the wet jacket and rolled up his sleeves.

She did the same.

"You'll have to assist," he told her. "Do you have any disinfectant in your duffel?"

"Uh, I have mouthwash, but not much. It's travel-size."

"We'll wash our hands in it. Give me something clean to dry off on."

She dug through her duffel for the items, poured some of the mouthwash in his cupped hands when she found the plastic container, then gave him a towel to dry on. She washed and dried her hands, too.

"Help her remove the slacks," he ordered, motioning for her to climb over the back seat.

Her heart pounded. She forced herself to breathe deeply as she knelt beside her sister. "Let's get these off," she said, eyeing the loose maternity pants.

"I'm...sorry." Janis clutched both of Alison's hands as a contraction started. When it was over, she continued, "I'm sorry for being so hateful to you. I was afraid you'd talk me into going back. I love Keith. I want to stay with him and...make a new life. Please understand. Ohh..."

The next contraction was longer, harder. Alison held Janis's hands. "I understand. It's all right."

Travis knelt next to Janis. "Let's see where we are."

Alison was grateful for his competent manner and calm tone. Looking at his drawn face, she knew—oh, yes, she knew!—how much this was going to cost. She could see the barriers slamming into place, hiding the vulnerability.

As soon as the contraction eased, she helped get the maternity pants and undergarments off. Travis told Janis to prop her knees up. He asked Alison to hold the flashlight.

"It's crowning," he murmured.

"What does that mean?" Alison asked.

"Ready or not, this baby is coming." He bent toward Janis. "Now we're going to have to work some.

When I tell you to push, I want you to hold your breath, grasp the back of your knees and push like crazy. Think you can do that?''

Janis nodded. "I think…so.''

"Should I stop?" Keith asked.

Even in the dim light, Alison could see the worry in his eyes and his fear for Janis, but she had no assurances that all would be well. For once, she didn't have any ideas on what to do.

"No,'' Travis said. "We need to get to the house. Beau should be there.''

Relief surged through Alison at the mention of the doctor but not for long. Janis doubled up and cried out as the next contraction began.

"Put that pillow and blanket behind her,'' Travis ordered Alison. He smiled at Janis. "Okay, it's time to push. Grab your knees and bear down as hard as you can.''

"What's happening?" Keith asked, risking a quick glance over his shoulder. "Is she okay?"

Holding the flashlight as steady as possible, Alison described what was happening as Travis worked with Janis. She was vaguely aware of heat flushing through her body and a sheen of perspiration breaking out all over her.

"Rest now,'' Travis said. He swiped over Janis's face, then his own, with a T-shirt. "Prepare something for the baby,'' he said to Alison.

She selected her nightshirt, not sure what she was preparing for.

"Okay," he murmured. "Big push. Take a deep breath. Grab those knees. Push."

Alison held her breath, too. A low, keening sound issued from Janis, then a cry as the baby came in a gush of effort and released breath.

"What was that?" Keith demanded, sounding frantic. "Is she okay?"

Travis ran a finger inside the baby's mouth, then flipped the baby over and swatted his rear. The infant gave a strangled snort, then his chest lifted in his first gulp of air and he let out a cry of indignation.

"You have a son," Alison said to Keith, tears burning her eyes. She blinked them away.

"Dental floss," Travis said. "You have some?"

Her fingers visibly shook as she got the floss out of her toiletry kit and handed it over.

"Mouthwash."

She poured some into his hand and over the floss. When she set the container aside, he held the baby out to her.

"Wipe him down with the T-shirt," he ordered.

While he tied off the umbilical cord and tidied up the birth scene, she dried the protesting infant on her nightshirt, then tucked another T-shirt around him for a diaper, then finally wrapped him in a fleece vest.

"Here, Mom," she said to Janis. "Meet your new son. Have you picked out a name yet?"

Janis's smile was wobbly. She cradled the baby in her arms. "Keith Jr."

''There's the ranch house,'' Keith announced. ''We're almost there.''

The relief was palpable in the truck. Alison smiled and blinked rapidly as her eyes misted over again. Her gaze was drawn to Travis. ''Thank you,'' she whispered. ''You were wonderful...*wonderful.*''

She'd never felt such a tide of love as she felt now. Sensitive to his every nuance, she was also aware of the darkness in his eyes and the way the skin stretched over his bones and the tic of a muscle in his jaw as he rolled the used towel and clothing up and stored them in a plastic bag he found by the rear door.

She laid a hand on his arm in apology. Somehow she felt responsible, as if she'd been the one to drag him into the drama of the birth scene.

He returned her gaze impassively, and she knew he'd withdrawn far into himself where he allowed no emotion and rejected any connection to what had just taken place. She removed her hand.

Keith had to stop at a gate. He jumped out, opened it and was back before Alison could volunteer.

''Leave it,'' Travis said when the younger man would have closed the gate behind them.

Keith drove to the lighted house. The rain had settled to a steady drizzle when Travis lifted Janis from the SUV and took her into the warm house. Alison followed with the baby, Keith right behind.

''What the—'' Uncle Nick began.

''Beau!'' Travis yelled.

''In the kitchen,'' the cousin replied.

"Janis had her baby in the car," Travis explained as Beau and Trevor appeared in the kitchen doorway, each holding a plate of toast and eggs.

Beau became all business. He thrust the plate at Trevor. "Put her in the Rose Room. I'll get my bag."

Alison trailed after Travis and Keith. Trevor, after putting the plates on a counter, followed behind her, then pulled the covers back when Travis paused beside the bed.

Beau entered with the black doctor's bag and several towels. "Thanks," he said to Travis. "You men can go. Uh, the father can stay. Alison, let me see the baby."

Travis and Trevor beat a fast retreat and closed the door after them. Beau checked the baby, who was now nodding off to sleep. He listened to the infant's heart and told her to wrap him back up. Then he turned to Janis.

After several minutes, he finished the medical exam and pronounced mother and son fit, then asked the parents about the Rh factor. "No problem there," he said upon finding Janis and Keith were both positives. "We can call an ambulance and have you taken to the hospital at the county seat, if you'd feel more comfortable there."

"Can't I stay here?" Janis asked in a teary voice.

Beau nodded. "It would take an ambulance an hour to get here and another hour to get back. Since you're doing fine, I don't see any reason to get out in the weather again." He spoke to Alison, who sat in a rocker. "Bring that boy over and let's see if he wants to eat."

Under Beau's coaching, Janis fed the baby his first meal. Next, Beau showed Keith how to burp the infant. The baby fell asleep against his father's shoulder.

Beau left and returned in a moment with a laundry basket lined with a blanket. "Here's his first bed."

Alison slipped from the room while they tucked the newcomer in. She paused in the hallway and pressed her hands over her eyes until she was sure of her composure, then she joined the men in the living room.

Trevor was in one chair, Uncle Nick in another. Travis wasn't with them.

"He went out," Trevor answered her unspoken question.

"He was marvelous. I don't know what Keith and Janis would have done without him."

"I think he needs to be alone just now," Uncle Nick said quietly. "He'll return when he's ready."

Glancing out the front window, she realized his truck was gone. She understood at once that he'd headed for the mountains and that he wouldn't be back, not for a while at any rate. He needed to let the old wounds rest.

She'd leaned on him many times since coming to the Seven Devils area. Closing her eyes for a second, she relived his strength, his innate gentleness that a woman could depend on. She wished he could have turned to her, but she hadn't expected it. Travis was too used to turning his anguish inward. He refused to need anyone.

"I'm sorry," she said, "but is there a place I can wash up? I need to shower and change into dry clothing."

Trevor was on his feet with an apology in an instant. "This way. I left your bag in here." He led her to a pretty bedroom along the same hallway as the Rose Room where Janis was. "The bathroom is across the hall. Uh, I'd better tell Keith he can use the other bedroom."

Alison closed the door and sank onto a chair at a pine desk. She didn't think Janis would need her, not with Keith and Beau taking care of her and the baby. She needed time alone.

After a hot shower, she did feel better. Dressed in clean clothing, she patted back a yawn, realized it was still early and decided to rest for an hour.

Hearing a muted cry next door, she smiled as a soft glow brightened her spirits. A baby. Little Janny's baby. She was an aunt. Wouldn't the folks be surprised to learn they were grandparents!

But that was Janis's story. She'd let her little sister tell it.

"'Happy birthday, Uncle Ni-ick, happy birthday to you.'"

Alison joined the Daltons in singing the traditional song that evening, Uncle Nick blew out the one big candle on his cake, then they all clapped. Veronica Dalton, called Roni by her family, cut the first slice and presented it to the old man.

Glancing around the dining-room table, Alison perused each person. Today she'd met the entire Dalton gang when they'd arrived for the birthday celebration.

Seth, the oldest, was odd man out in this family of blue-eyed, pale-skinned siblings and cousins. He was dark-eyed with black hair and swarthy skin. Zack was next in age, then Beau and the twins, while the lone girl cousin was the youngest at twenty-five.

Janis and Keith took part from the living room where the new mother rested on the sofa, her attentive husband beside her. The baby was asleep in the Rose Room.

The little family had gone into town with Beau for a more thorough checkup in his office that morning. All were fine. Uncle Nick had suggested they stay at his place until tomorrow in case they needed to ask Beau's advice. The couple had accepted the invitation gratefully.

After everyone had a slice of cake and ice cream and were seated in the living room, Uncle Nick spoke, "A man's family means a lot to him on special days like this. I'm glad you could all make it." He smiled at Janis. "It's especially nice to welcome a new life into the world. The boy and I share the same birthday so we'll have to celebrate together every year."

A murmur of laughter passed over the room. Uncle Nick thanked them for his gifts. Alison had given him a cookbook that had recipes for using wild plants that grew in the area, while his kin had given him clothing and personal items.

Only Travis was absent from the happy scene.

Night fell softly on the land. Seth and Roni left for Boise, deciding to return that night due to the additional guests in the house. Zack went to his place in town. After Keith and Janis retired to the Rose Room, Alison watched the TV news with Trevor, Beau and Uncle Nick.

It was only after the old man went to bed that Trevor spoke to her. "Why don't you go to him?"

She didn't pretend to misunderstand. "I don't think he wants anyone right now."

"He's hurting," Beau said.

She nodded. She'd seen his eyes before he'd disappeared from the house. The birth had brought back memories of all he'd lost. He would have to come to terms with the grief—and his guilt—by himself.

Trevor spoke again. "He's probably gone to the cabin since it's stocked and closer than any other place."

She inhaled slowly, carefully. "Wherever he is, he'll have to get over his grief alone. No one can do it for him."

"But you could remind him of all that he's giving up by staying locked in the past," Beau suggested.

"He isn't locked in the past. He simply doesn't want a future. Maybe he never will. Or maybe he hasn't met the woman who will reawaken his dreams.''

She wasn't that woman. Last night had given her false hopes, but the morning had dispelled such foolishness.

''You're as stubborn as he said,'' Trevor muttered. ''Both of you are. Kidnapping again?'' he asked his cousin.

Beau thought it over. ''How about it?'' he asked her. ''Are you afraid to give it another try?''

Her heart set up a harsh beat that echoed through her like a danger signal. She shook her head.

''Good. Let's go.'' Trevor grabbed a raincoat from the front closet and glanced at her as if assessing the size.

''No, no,'' she protested. ''I'm not going to him.''

The twin looked disappointed. He put the raincoat away. Beau announced he was going to bed and left them. Lights flashed outside.

''Little brother has returned,'' Trevor told her.

With a grin, he crossed the room and plopped down beside her on the sofa. Before Alison could figure out his intent, he put an arm around her and hauled her close.

''Don't,'' she said, startled by his action but not alarmed. There was too much friendly mischief in his eyes.

''This worked once before. Trav and Julie had a fight, the only one I ever knew them to have. I took her to the senior prom. That woke him up.''

"It won't work this time," she managed to say just as Trevor kissed her.

Cold air swirled around them as the door opened. Trevor lifted his head and frowned at his twin. "Bad timing, bro," he complained lightly.

"Sorry," Travis said. "I'm just passing through."

He didn't glance her way, but walked past them, down the hall and into his bedroom. The door closed.

Trevor cursed softly. "It's worse than I thought."

She pulled away and stood. "I know you're concerned about him, but please leave me out of it."

For once there was no merriment in Trevor's eyes. "Maybe you're right. Maybe no one can reach him now. I don't know...the way he looked at you when you held the baby...I thought...but maybe not."

He was still trying to figure it out when she retreated to her room. Through the wall, she heard the faint cry of the baby. Little Keith's first day had been exciting.

She sensed the passing of time as the fall of sand through an hourglass. Sometimes it seemed fast, sometimes slow. The years passed. Before she knew it, she would be middle-aged, then old. Last night had taught her something—she didn't want to spend her life alone.

"She has a slight fever," Beau announced, putting the thermometer and blood pressure cuff away. "I think you'd better stay here for a couple of days," he told Janis.

"We have several new horses to see to," she protested.

"I'll go to the ranch and take care of them," Keith told her. He appealed to Alison. "Can you stay with her?"

"Yes, Alison must stay," Janis at once agreed. She pressed her lips together, then gazed at Alison, who was in the rocking chair with the baby. "Would you?" she asked with surprising humbleness, her smile hesitant.

Alison smiled at her sister. "Of course. I want more time with this little darling."

"Good." Beau took a throat swab to culture in case of strep throat, which had plagued Janis as a child. "I'll call when I have the results."

Sunday afternoon passed quietly after that. Alison and Janis had a long talk after Beau and Keith left. Janis shared her dream of making a successful ranch with Keith. Alison mentioned her desire to go back into teaching.

"Do it," Janis urged. "I dare you!"

Alison wandered outside after Janis and little Keith fell asleep. The weather had cleared on Saturday afternoon and today was as beautiful as polished crystal.

On an impulse, she walked through the woods to the unfinished house. Instead of going inside, she sat on the porch and let the quiet seep into her soul.

The past two days had been tumultuous, filled with fears for her sister and the child. The sweet tenderness between Keith and Janis as they cared for their son, as well as his concern at her illness, tugged at her heart. She observed the bonds growing moment by moment between the young couple as they shared life.

Love could be a beautiful thing.

Janis had finally called home with no urging from her big sister. The parents had naturally been astounded, but Janis had made the delivery in the truck into an adventure and her failure to tell them of the pregnancy a surprise she'd planned from the beginning.

A rustle in the grass drew her attention to the sunlit clearing. Travis crossed the springy turf and took a seat on the steps, keeping a couple of feet between them.

"Beau says your sister is running a fever," he said.

"Yes. He put her on antibiotics."

"Good."

She saw him inhale deeply and release the breath as if relieved. "I'm sorry we're imposing on your family," she said. "Beau suggested we not move Janis yet."

"It's okay." He gripped the edge of the porch.

"You were wonderful during the birth," she continued, needing to thank him, but not sure if he would let her.

"I took classes…we did, Julie and I."

She nodded. "I assumed you did."

His smile was beautiful, and so sad it shattered her heart. She looked away.

After a pause, he continued, "We went to Council once a week—Beau insisted—and learned to breathe and watched some videos. At first I didn't think I could go through with it, but then I looked at the other men and realized we were all scared out of our boots over assisting in birth."

His laughter was brief, painful in its irony. She held her smile in place with an effort. Not for anything would she let him see her pity.

"But we had been in on the conception, so it was only fair that we follow through on the rest." He paused and his smile became real. "My grandmother told me the first Dalton here had to help his wife. There wasn't anyone else."

She nodded, envisioning the ranch house, which had been a log cabin then, seeing the couple struggle to make a living from the rugged land and bringing their children, literally, into the world by their own efforts. It all seemed so endearing.

Travis continued, "So we waited for the birth of our son and built the house. Our plan was to have it done before the baby came."

"But it didn't work out that way."

"No," he said quietly. "It didn't work out that way."

She waited, wanting him to go on, but not pushing. This was his story. She'd let him tell it in his own way, just as she'd learned she must do with her little sister.

Perhaps she was growing up, too.

Finally he finished in a deadpan voice. "She woke me one night, moaning and in pain. I thought she was having a nightmare at first. She was, only it was real. I called ahead and started for the hospital, but I knew…before we got there…that we weren't going to make it."

A jay scolded another from the cedar tree at the edge of the clearing. The breeze rippled across the long blades of grass, forming it into waves as if it were a green sea.

"I'm sorry," Alison said. There were no other words.

"Yeah, so was I. It didn't help. She was dead and I was the one who did it."

Pity wrung her heart. "No, you didn't. It was a tragedy, but it wasn't your fault."

"Whose was it if not mine?" he asked with the finality of unshakable belief. "I knew, on that long miserable trip, that it was hopeless. She tried to be brave, to hide the pain, but I knew."

"You couldn't have—"

But maybe he did, she decided, looking into his eyes. They seemed filled with ages-old knowledge. At any rate, he'd taken the blame upon himself and there it resided, buried in pain too deep for her to reach.

"So you're never entitled to happiness again," she concluded as darkness gathered inside her.

"Happiness?" The planes of his handsome face hardened until the bones jutted against the skin. "I don't want it. I don't want the responsibility."

"Yes," she murmured. "It's hard to let go."

His gaze was sharp. "Of what?"

"Grief. Guilt."

Standing, he faced her. "What do you know of it?" he asked so softly it was scary. "What can you, viewing life from your gilded cage, possibly know?"

He strode across the waving sea of grass and disappeared into the forest, blending into his surroundings like a creature of the mountains, untamed and angry and so very dangerous because he was so very wounded.

Time. Only time would heal him. Maybe.

But she wouldn't wait. Tomorrow, if all went well with her sister and nephew, she would leave.

Time. It was all she had to fill the emptiness.

"Loneliness," she said at last. "I know loneliness."

Chapter 13

Travis whacked the nail holding the hinge on the new barn door with the hammer, then cursed when it bent.

"You have to hit the nail straight on, bro," Trevor advised, coming up behind him.

Travis yanked the nail out, threw it on the floor and drove in another with three strikes. He ignored his brother, hoping he'd go away.

No such luck.

"Tomorrow's Saturday. You're free, aren't you?" Trevor continued.

"So?"

"You could go down to Boise. There's a fancy political fund-raiser going on, I understand."

"Huh." Travis pounded another nail.

Haunted by memories, he'd worked every spare minute of every day. Oddly, the memories were recent ones, not the old ones that had taunted him with failure.

"I happen to have a ticket," Trevor continued.

He whirled on his brother. "Butt out," he ordered.

Trevor shrugged. "You're a fool if you don't go."

"For what? What would be the point?"

"Your future." Trevor sat on a sawhorse and gave him a hard stare. "Ask her to marry you. She might say yes."

The abyss rolled uncomfortably. Travis saw no need to see Allison and ask her anything.

"Funny," his twin continued, "I thought your marriage was a good one, that you were happy. I guess not."

"It was. I wouldn't trade the three years I had with Julie for a million dollars in the bank," he said stiffly.

"Even if you'd known at the time what was to come?"

"Sweet Jesus," he muttered, a prayer for strength not to hit his intrusive twin with the hammer. He flung it on the ground. "I don't need this."

"If marriage was so great, why are you such a coward about trying it again?"

"Get out of here before I…" He couldn't think of a worthy retaliation. Fighting was stupid.

"Before you let the chance of a lifetime slip right through your fingers? Think about that. Think about what Julie would want for you." He laid a ticket on the sawhorse. "Zack asked me to take over the poacher watch, so I'm heading for the hills." He left in his truck.

Travis picked up the ticket, intending to tear it into pieces. After a long minute, he stuffed it in his shirt pocket and got back to work.

As he picked up the hammer, the sun reflected off it and into his eyes, dazzling him for a second.

In the shiny metal, he saw his face, thinner than it had been two weeks ago when Alison packed and Beau drove her back to the city. Staring into his eyes, he saw only darkness, a calm darkness. That was the way he wanted it.

The sun caught the edge of the hammer and blinded him once more. Through the reflected radiance he saw something…a golden aura that started his heart to pounding…the enchanting outline of a woman… He knew she was smiling…and that she held her arms out to him…to welcome him to the light…

Did he dare step into the circle of brilliance?

"Yes, right there," Alison said.

The men put the enormous ice sculpture in the center of the table. The frozen mermaid erupting from the waves was beautiful. She'd watched the chef carve the mythical figure, fascinated by his skill.

After directing the men in arranging the flowers around the base of the mermaid, she glanced around one more time, satisfied that all was being done as planned.

"The red carpet is out," Greg, one of the young movers and shakers who worked for her father, announced.

"Good. Thanks for helping with the details."

Glancing at her watch, she saw it was time to go to her room. She found it easier to stay at the hotel rather than run back and forth to her family home, which was a distance from town, during events such as this.

"Can you keep an eye on things here for a few minutes?" she asked. "I need to get dressed."

"Sure."

She wasn't unaware of the admiration in his eyes. As she rode the elevator to her floor, she wondered why she'd never fallen for someone like him. He was handsome, well-spoken, intelligent and ambitious.

Because she'd known her married life would be like the one she'd been born into? Fund-raising. Campaigning. Months in the nation's capital. It wasn't a terrible life, but it wasn't the one she wanted for her children.

What children?

Rolling her eyes at her ridiculous musing, she quickly showered and dressed in a pale blue–green evening outfit of silk chiffon with a satin slip and cummerbund waist. The sheer sleeves were pleated and gathered into satin bands that fastened with pearl buttons at her wrists.

Her hair had already been set into an artful Grecian cascade of curls at the back of her head, with flirty tendrils floating at her temples and nape. With a simple pearl necklace and earrings and an iridescent sheen in her eye shadow and powder, she was ready.

This was an important function, the kickoff dinner for her father's drive to be governor. And the last event she would plan for him. She'd been accepted to teach at Lost Valley High starting in September.

Her insides clenched into a ball of uncertainty. Not for the first time, she wondered if she was doing the right thing. Maybe her heart would be broken, but that foolish organ was set on one of the seven devils who lived in the mountains, Travis Dalton by name.

Amelia had already promised her a room at the B&B for a very reasonable price. Heading for the elevator, Alison admitted finding an apartment in a small town had proven more difficult than in the city, which was going through a boom in construction at present.

Entering the ballroom, she made a last sweep of the room and saw that all was in order. The dais for the six-piece combo was in place. Spotlights highlighted the dessert tables, while the rest of the ornate room was cast in a soft glow. All of the one hundred tables was decorated with a lovely floral arrangement that some lucky person at each one would take home as a gift.

"All is in order," Greg assured her, coming to her side as soon as he spotted her. "You look beautiful."

She hardly noticed the compliment. "Thanks. Do

you think it's too warm in here? The ice sculpture seems to be melting fast.''

''No, it's just right.'' He chucked her under the chin when they reached their table. ''Quit worrying.''

His seat was next to hers, she saw. Probably her mother's doing. Her parents were at the main VIP table. The state political manager and her husband were to preside at a second. She and Greg were partnered at the third.

She made herself look at him, really look. He was successful and well on his way in his career as an economic adviser in government affairs. He would probably run for office someday. Some woman would be lucky to get him.

She wasn't that woman.

Along with a new knowledge of herself had come an insight into her family. Her father was ambitious, but it was her mother who directed the family in serving that ambition. With her father's unspoken consent.

A husband and wife should be supportive of each other, but that didn't mean manipulating your children into living their lives focused on the same goals.

People were individuals and had to find their own reasons for being, thus her move to Lost Valley. If it didn't work out, maybe she would move on. All that could be decided later.

That was another thing she'd learned. She didn't have to have a plan for every moment, with a contingency plan to back up the first.

That elusive plan B.

If people could look inside her, they would see an odd mixture of sadness and joy. She smiled as she recalled her sojourn in the mountains. She'd found more than her errant sibling.

Peace. Happiness. Love. They had seemed within her grasp for a time...a very short time.

Laying her evening bag on the table, she went over her list one more time, then spoke to the catering manager. Everything was proceeding as it should.

Travis stood near the entrance to the ballroom and watched the activity. The attendees reminded him of ants rushing about in an anthill, busy as could be. The room wasn't crowded by any means, nor hot, but he felt stifled and uncomfortable.

Taking a quick check on what the other men were wearing, he saw dark suits were the order of the evening. Good thing. He didn't own a tux. Neither did anyone in his family that he knew of. Again he wondered if he was in his right mind for coming.

This was Alison's world, and it didn't take a genius to know it wasn't his. Not that he had anything against the people here. Politicians were as necessary as cops.

He dodged the reception line where Senator Harvey, his wife, Alison and another man welcomed people with a gracious manner, completely at ease with the task. By holding a side door for a waiter, then entering behind the man, he ducked into the huge room where a couple hundred glamorous and influential people were gathered.

Glancing at his ticket, he found a matching table number in the middle of the room, two rows behind the VIP tables. He chose a chair where he could keep an eye on the front and accepted a glass of wine from a waiter.

Dinner was served on time. He had to admit the meal was good. The beef fillet was tender, the chicken in a wine sauce delicate, the vegetables crisp.

After the tables were cleared, Alison's father gave a brief talk and thanked them for coming. He announced his candidacy for governor. The audience stood and cheered. Then Alison invited the guests to visit the dessert ''stations'' located around the room.

Travis's breath froze in his lungs at his first direct view at her. She looked like a princess, one made of ice like the sculpture in the middle of the room. Her dress was as filmy as sea foam and the pale color of a tropical ocean.

She was everything he'd dreamed of the past two weeks and looked as remote as a mermaid on an ice floe. He swallowed hard as an ache formed in his chest.

The low background music stopped and a group of musicians took their places onstage.

He'd noted the guy hovering close to Alison all evening, apparently with the approval of her family. The senator had clapped the younger man on the shoulder in a friendly gesture and Alison's mother had embraced him like a long-lost son earlier.

Glancing around the ballroom, Travis knew Alison had done the planning and supervising of the event. One of the hotel managers approached as he watched and consulted with her. She discussed the problem, then smiled and nodded.

Travis's heart went into overdrive. What the hell was he doing here at a five-hundred-dollar-a-plate function? He counted the tables and did the math. Her father stood to raise a cool quarter-million dollars tonight for his campaign, minus the cost of the food and trappings.

Deciding to skip dessert and the rest of the event, he headed for the door. Unfortunately, everyone else also stood and started milling about. He was stalled halfway to his goal by several men who greeted each other heartily.

To either side of that group, people blocked his progress. He did an about-face, intending to try one of the side doors. His eyes met startled green ones.

Everything in him shifted and brightened, as if the sun came up at that moment.

Standing in a circle of light, she was as radiant as a crystal, reminding him of the first time he saw her, that day in the forest. He'd known then she was going to be trouble. He should have heeded the warning.

She blinked, then nodded without smiling. He returned her acknowledgment with a dip of his head.

His insides burned. An ache sprang into being as

he surveyed her against this rich, luxuriant background. He wished he'd never come here. Listening to his twin had always gotten him into trouble.

Three chatting women came between him and her. When they had passed, Alison was engaged in conversation with her escort and an older, prosperous-looking couple. He realized it was a senator from an adjoining state.

Desperate for a way out, he wound a path through the crowd and came upon the ice sculpture.

The mermaid resembled Alison in her cool, remote beauty. However, Alison wasn't cold or remote. She was warm and passionate and responsive.

The ache bloomed into a piercing pain that reached all the way to some lost part of him. A woman wearing diamonds at her ears and throat swept by him. Turning, he nearly ran another woman over. His hands went to her shoulders.

"Sorry," he said and stepped back. His heart stopped, just stopped.

"That's okay," Alison said, her heart skipping several beats as he released his hold on her. "Have you tried any of the desserts yet?"

"Uh, no. I was just leaving."

She struggled with a smile, forcing it to stay in place. Why had he come? Why was he leaving?

"I'm going to try the cream tarts. Sure you can't be tempted?" She gave him a flirty glance because that was easier than letting herself cry.

His chest moved as he drew a deep breath. "Yes,"

he said in an oddly resigned voice. "I can be tempted."

When his eyes met hers, she looked for answers to his presence there, but it was like looking at a wall. She handed him a clear crystal plate and took one for herself. They selected a variety of artfully decorated concoctions.

"This way," she said, leading him to her table. "How is Uncle Nick?"

"Fine." Travis took the seat next to her. "What happened to your date?"

She looked puzzled. "Oh, Greg. He isn't a date. He works for my father. Right now, he'll be pressing the flesh, as they say in political circles."

Travis nodded. He watched her take a bite of tart. He went into meltdown when she licked a smear of cream off her lower lip. He couldn't look away.

"Don't," she protested, her lashes fluttering down over her eyes.

He wanted to take a bite out of her. He wanted to kiss her breathless. He wanted to grab her up and run off to someplace quiet and soft.

Near them the woman draped in diamonds laughed. The stones sent off flashes like Fourth of July sparklers.

Travis took a breath. "I came here with a crazy idea," he began, then stopped. He'd never known he was a coward.

"Yes?" Alison couldn't help the hope that surged

in her. She wished everyone would be quiet…or better, just disappear.

"I thought I'd ask you to marry me," he said doggedly, "but I didn't realize what I'd be asking you to leave behind." He gestured at the opulent ballroom and the distinguished guests.

Alison couldn't breathe. She couldn't have heard him right. "Marry?" she repeated.

He shrugged. "Forget it. It was just a thought."

Her heart dropped to her toes. Then anger rushed over her. "No, I won't forget it." She glared at him. "Did you mean it or not?"

He glared right back, then his gaze softened. "I meant it. Crazy, huh?"

"I really wish you'd take me away from all this," she said. Happiness made her giddy. She laughed. "I'm a mountain woman, and I'm much happier there."

Memories flashed between them. Travis felt a glow start deep inside, like a candle in the wind, holding out against the storm. "Can we go somewhere private?"

"I have a room here."

He took her hand and helped her out of the chair. "So do I, but I don't trust myself with you."

"*I* trust you."

"You shouldn't," he muttered, leading the way toward a side door.

"Alison, where are you going?"

Alison blinked at her mother. "Home," she said and knew she didn't mean here.

"You can't leave—"

"Greg has everything under control," Senator Harvey interrupted smoothly, appearing at their side. He winked at Travis and Alison, then told his wife, "I'll circulate and find out which way the political winds are blowing."

"Thank you," Alison murmured.

"Go on, you two. My blessings," he whispered.

"What is going on?" Virginia Harvey demanded.

"A wedding, I'd say." The senator grinned. "This will be good for my political future. After all, the public loves a romance."

"Well, yes," her mother said, her face lighting up.

Alison couldn't keep the smile off her face. It radiated from her heart. She kissed her mother and father on the cheek, then spoke to her beloved. "Come on."

Travis nodded at the older couple, then followed his love out the door. His love. The words made him nervous. If he said them aloud, The Fates might get jealous.

He realized that was a coward's thought and pushed it away. The glow increased to a shimmering radiance. He'd realized during the long night that he couldn't continue without her warmth.

She led him to a service elevator. In less than five minutes they were in her room. He eyed the bed, then turned to her. There were things to be talked out between them.

"I stopped by the police department this morning and picked up an application. They need men since the town started booming as a new Silicon Valley."

She shook her head. "I start as a teacher at Lost Valley High in September. I'll be taking over for another teacher who's going out on maternity leave."

"What?"

"I'm going to—"

"I heard you. When was I going to know about this?"

"Well, I assumed I'd run into you in town."

He laid his hands on her shoulders and gave her a little shake. "I've been going crazy since you left. I devised a million plans on how we could be together and a million reasons for why we couldn't." He paused then added softly, "I'm not very good at cherishing and protecting."

She stroked the thick dark hair from his forehead. "Yes, you are. Look how you helped me. Look how you helped Janis and the baby. Life happens to everyone. We can't change that."

He touched her dress and ran a finger along the neckline. "You're silk and satin. I'm denim."

She heard the questions. She'd felt the same doubts while she waited to hear about the teaching position, afraid he wouldn't want her, that the attraction was only sexual on his part or a misunderstanding on hers.

"Money and lifestyle are not issues between us," she said. "Love is. And the future. I want children."

Travis saw the undaunted certainty in her eyes and was humbled by her courage. He knew he had to be as brave. "I do love you. I think I have from that first meeting in the mountains when you were so determined to carry out your search, no matter what it took."

She nodded, not at all surprised. "I fell in love with you when you shared your tent and food with me, a little more each time it happened."

"Don't lie."

"There was an attraction from the first," she reminded him. "We just had to work through all the other stuff."

Her smile was gentle, her gaze direct and clear. He knew her to be a loyal and honorable woman. "The average net earnings of a rancher is forty thousand. In a good year." He had to be fair and make sure she knew what she was getting.

"The average starting salary of a teacher is less than thirty thousand." She grinned.

So did he. He couldn't help it, not when she looked at him like that. The doubts faded. He drew her into his arms. Maybe he didn't deserve it, but he was getting another chance. No way he'd let it go, not now.

"How soon can we be married? Where do you want to go for a honeymoon?" he demanded.

"The cabin? It's already stocked."

He groaned, then chuckled. "My brother will think he brought all this about."

"Uncle Nick told me the abduction was his idea."

Travis, about to kiss her delectable mouth, stopped. "What?"

"He confessed all my last day there and apologized to me. He felt really bad about everything."

"That old codger," Travis growled. "I ought to…" He couldn't think of any retaliation worthy of the old man's conniving ways, well, maybe a million dollars, but he didn't have that.

Alison laid her fingertips over his lips. "We'll thank him and tell him he was absolutely right."

She snuggled close and the warmth in him became a threatening volcano.

"Would you kiss me now?" she asked.

It was a request he couldn't refuse. Later there would be other things to talk about. He ran a finger along the edge of the silk dress. "You look like a princess."

Alison knew what he was thinking. She unzipped the dress, stepped out of it and flung it on a chair. The slip followed. Her heart danced at the fire in his eyes. She pulled the pins out of her hair, one by one, until the strands slipped down around her face.

"I'm simply a woman, my love, one who was lonely until she met someone wonderful."

Then she melted in his arms, demanding his kiss. He gave her his all—body, heart and soul.

Much later, she laughed softly.

"What?" he murmured.

"I was thinking about our children. Will they be little devils or angels?"

"Some of both. They'll give us grief and they'll give us joy. We'll weather it." He touched her face and saw the glow in her, felt it inside him. "Together."

Together, they'd teach their children to be decent, caring people, to fulfill their own destinies and to find a home wherever their hearts led them.

Alison knew she'd been lucky. She'd gone into the mountains to find her sister. She'd found adventure and romance. She'd also found her true love, just as Janis had.

"It was worth it," she said aloud.

Travis raised himself to his elbow and peered into her eyes, marveling at the love he saw there, all for him. "What was?"

"The journey into the Seven Devils Mountains."

He had to agree. He'd faced his own demons there, and he'd found his treasure. Not gold. His true treasure.

That of the heart.

* * * * *

The SEVEN DEVILS *are getting matched up if Uncle Nick has his way! So what happens when Zack meets his match? Find out in* Showdown!, *coming this June from Silhouette Special Edition.*

♥ SILHOUETTE®
SPECIAL EDITION™

AVAILABLE FROM 16TH APRIL 2004

A BILLIONAIRE AND A BABY Marie Ferrarella
The Mum Squad

Sherry Campbell knows more about St John 'Sin-Jin' Adair than he's happy with. He wants privacy, but he also wants to kiss her into next year...not to mention become part of her family!

QUINN'S WOMAN Susan Mallery
Hometown Heartbreakers

Quinn Reynolds was knocked head over heels—literally—by DJ Monroe. She never let anyone close—then she fell for the dangerous and magnetic paramilitary expert...and he knew he was in trouble.

FAITH, HOPE AND FAMILY Gina Wilkins
The McClouds of Mississippi

Only one man could rekindle the passion Deborah McCloud had sworn to leave behind: Dylan Smith. But would she be able to mend the mistakes she'd made seven years earlier?

FUGITIVE FIANCÉE Kristin Gabriel
Maitland Maternity

Rugged Garrett Lord is tired of women flinging themselves at him—and then he finds Mimi Casville in his barn in full wedding regalia...she's sweet, she's sexy and she's hiding something...

THE UNEXPECTED WEDDING GUEST
Patricia McLinn
Something Old, Something New

Suz Grant used to have a crush on Max Trevetti, but he'd always acted like a big brother. Now Max was suddenly behaving strangely. Could it be that he was feeling more than brotherly affection?

CATTLEMAN'S HONOUR Pamela Toth
Winchester Brides

Emily Major was looking for a quiet life for herself and her son, but Adam Winchester was determined to win her heart. Just how far would Adam go to make her his?

AVAILABLE FROM 16TH APRIL 2004

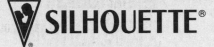 **SILHOUETTE**®

Sensation™

Passionate and thrilling romantic adventures

TO LOVE A THIEF Merline Lovelace
LAST SEEN... Carla Cassidy
SEVEN DAYS TO FOREVER Ingrid Weaver
IN TOO DEEP Sharon Mignerey
WHEN NIGHT FALLS Jenna Mills
LAURA AND THE LAWMAN Shelley Cooper

Intrigue™

Breathtaking romantic suspense

INTIMATE STRANGERS Rebecca York
TOUGH AS NAILS Jackie Manning
HEIR TO SECRET MEMORIES Mallory Kane
THE ROOKIE Julie Miller

Superromance™

*Enjoy the drama, explore the emotions,
experience the relationship*

BECAUSE OF THE BABY Anne Haven
LOST BUT NOT FORGOTTEN Roz Denny Fox
CHILD OF HER DREAMS Joan Kilby
WONDERS NEVER CEASE Debra Salonen

Desire™ 2-in-1

Passionate, dramatic love stories

WHERE'S THERE SMOKE... Barbara McCauley
BEAUTY & THE BLUE ANGEL Maureen Child

MAROONED WITH A MILLIONAIRE Kristi Gold
THE GENTRYS: ABBY Linda Conrad

TYCOON FOR AUCTION Katherine Garbera
SLEEPING WITH THE PLAYBOY Julianne MacLean

0404/23b

SILHOUETTE®

SPECIAL EDITION™

presents

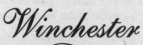

Winchester

Brides

By Pamela Toth

I**T TAKES A SPECIAL KIND OF WOMAN TO TAME
THESE IRRESISTIBLE BACHELORS!**

Cattleman's Honour

(May 2004)

Man Behind the Badge

(June 2004)

A Winchester Homecoming

(July 2004)

0404/SH/LC86

4 FREE

books and a surprise gift!

We would like to take this opportunity to thank you for reading this Silhouette® book by offering you the chance to take FOUR more specially selected titles from the Special Edition™ series absolutely FREE! We're also making this offer to introduce you to the benefits of the Reader Service™—

- ★ FREE home delivery
- ★ FREE gifts and competitions
- ★ FREE monthly Newsletter
- ★ Exclusive Reader Service offers
- ★ Books available before they're in the shops

Accepting these FREE books and gift places you under no obligation to buy, you may cancel at any time, even after receiving your free shipment. Simply complete your details below and return the entire page to the address below. *You don't even need a stamp!*

YES! Please send me 4 free Special Edition books and a surprise gift. I understand that unless you hear from me, I will receive 6 superb new titles every month for just £2.99 each, postage and packing free. I am under no obligation to purchase any books and may cancel my subscription at any time. The free books and gift will be mine to keep in any case.

E4ZED

Ms/Mrs/Miss/Mr ....Initials..................................
BLOCK CAPITALS PLEASE

Surname ....

Address ....

....

....Postcode..................................

Send this whole page to:
UK: FREEPOST CN81, Croydon, CR9 3WZ
EIRE: PO Box 4546, Kilcock, County Kildare (stamp required)